C000163983

POWER

POWER

An anthology of short stories by women from Wales

Edited by

ELIN AP HYWEL

HONNO MODERN FICTION

Published by Honno
'Ailsa Craig', Heol y Cawl, Dinas Powys,
South Glamorgan, Wales, CF6 4AH.

First Impression 1998

© *The Authors 1998*

British Library Cataloguing in Publication Data

Power
1. Title

ISBN 1 870206 26 6

All rights reserved

Published with the financial support of the
Arts Council of Wales

Acknowledgements

Cover illustration and design by Jo Hughes

Typeset and printed in Wales by Gwasg Dinefwr, Llandybïe

CONTENTS

FOREWORD

Welcome to the second Honno anthology of short stories by women from Wales. I hope you will find something – indeed, many things – here to enjoy. When I was choosing the stories to include in 'Power', trying to decide what my criteria should be, I had the sudden image of a handbag – a compendious kind of bag, the sort of hold-all in which you carry all the equipment of your daily life and from which anything – serviceable, stern, melancholy or just plain silly – might emerge: a paperclip, a tax bill, a love letter, or a suspender belt.

So there are stories of all kinds in this book. Stout stories, like Kay Brylewski's 'Teacher', with a beginning, a middle and an end; stories like Clare Morgan's lovely, elliptical 'Living Memory' which strain the short story form a bit at its seams. Stories, such as Madeline Mayne's 'Parties in Bridgend', about little girls and old women. Stories, like 'A Wild Boy' by Christine Harrison, about young men. Stories about middle-aged men and old men too, about office cleaners and office workers, sad aunts and security guards. Stories, in short, about people and the relationships between them and other people.

When Honno's first collection, *Luminous and Forlorn*, appeared in 1994, it sold out surprisingly quickly proving, as we had suspected, that there was a thirst for a book of this kind. Rather than reprinting the first anthology, however, we decided to move on and publish a second. Although we realized – half-way through the process of producing *Luminous and Forlorn* – that this would be the first-ever collection of short stories exclusively by women from Wales, it didn't aim to be definitive. (That rôle being far more appropriate to books such as the forthcoming *The View across the Valley,* where Jane Aaron has gathered together short fiction by women from Wales spanning the nineteenth century and the first half of the 20th.)

It was meant, rather, to be an acknowledgement of the fact that we still feel women writers in Wales need a chance to see their work in print; that short fiction is often the medium of choice for women writers (writing full-length fiction being exhausting for anybody, especially if they're madly samba-ing between work and childcare); that the short story, thanks to magazines such as *Cambrensis* and the *New Welsh Review,* and the Academy's Rhys Davies Award is an increasingly popular form in Wales; and that the best way to introduce new writers to the public is in the company of other writers who have published before. We're happy that at least three of the authors in this book – Susan Morgan, Shelagh Weeks and Janet Thomas – are seeing their work in print for the first time.

That, too, was why I chose to give it the title *Power:* power, not only in the sense of the power people have over other people, but also the power they have within themselves. Things are changing, glory be, but the term 'women's fiction' has been used so often to belittle writing by women, shooing it into a ghetto concerned only with 'women's things', where emotions are all mixed up with hair remover and jampot covers and of about equal importance, that it is still a term women are wary of using. I hope that the readers of this collection will welcome these 'women's fictions' and enjoy the power of lives both ordinary and strange.

Elin ap Hywel
Cardiff, Autumn 1998

ACKNOWLEDGEMENTS

The following stories have already been broadcast or published elsewhere: Elizabeth Baines's stories have appeared in the collections *Everyday Matters* (Sheba Feminist Press, 1983) and *Northern Lights* (Lancaster House, 1994); 'Homecoming' by Christine Harrison in *Woman's Own* and on BBC Radio 4; 'Living Memory' by Clare Morgan in her collection *An Affair of the Heart* (Seren, 1996). 'The Game' and 'The Word' by Nia Williams have both appeared in the short story magazine *Cambrensis*.

POWER

~

Elizabeth Baines

Today my powers increased.

Next door's cat was picking its way along the fence and I sent it my beams. It stopped. It couldn't move. One paw half-up and its tail stuck in one place in the air.

We were in the garden because Mum was on the phone again. 'Why don't you play outside?' she said, as soon as she'd answered it, so we knew it was Cassie, and she'd be on the phone for half an hour or even an hour, saying the same things over and over, every so often dropping to a whisper – she thinks we can't hear, she thinks we don't know she's talking about Dad. And sighing: the way she makes a flat hiss and it squashes all the air around so your lungs get squashed too.

We stood in the doorway and didn't go, we didn't want to. She looked irritated and a bit upset. Then she said, 'Go on, there's good little girls,' in a pleady question not an order. And somehow then my chest felt lighter, and that was when I guessed my powers had grown.

'OK,' I said, and we whipped around and went.

As we stepped outside, the cat leapt up the fence towards us in a swoop of orange as though he just couldn't help it, and came face to face with us, and almost toppled on the edge, his yellow eyes wide with shock.

He tried to resist. He turned away, stuck his tail in the air and showed us his pink bum-hole and started tip-toeing towards the shed roof.

And then I did it, and he stopped short, right where he was. I let him go again. He turned and stared at me, astonished. He waited, to see if I was going to do it again. He turned away carefully, trying it out. I let him, for now.

After that we went off over the road to the building site where they've uncovered an old rubbish-tip and where we're not supposed to go. It's all forlorn there when the workmen have gone home and you go looking for bits of glass and blue-and-white crockery. If you lie on your belly the diggers rear up like great dragons and the white sky tips towards you in a scary way.

She never suspected. When we got back she was still on the phone, still on about Dad.

We haven't seen him for weeks.

She goes on and on:

Well, you know what he's like, Cass. He's hooked on that job. And can you blame him – he's so good at it. He's made that firm millions with the Dine-Air account. All the clients are fighting to have him on their campaigns. And I'd be a damn fool if I didn't accept that it puts temptation in his way. Artists, actresses and models – they all think he's God's gift. Oh no, I've long got used to **that**. *He's always been quite open, and none of them have ever meant a thing.*

But **this** *one, this time: for God's sake, he says it's a* **passion**! *A continuity girl, for heaven's sake. Now if it were one of the copywriters or a creative designer. But he says he's in* **love**! *It makes you want to puke. Well, it has to be something else. Something to do with* **him**. *Yes, I know what you think, Cass: mid-life crisis. But I think it's a bit more complicated than that. There's a whole load of unresolved stuff, you know, to do with the kids. He's besotted with those kids. Yet it clashes with all his dearly-held principles of freedom and hanging loose. The kids have* *opened up an area he simply hadn't accounted for. I think that's the reason he's keeping away. He knows if he comes back once it will break his resolve.*

She's suddenly silent. Then:

Are you listening on that extension, Emma? Put it down!

She's on the phone again while we're watching *Beauty and the Beast* in my room. I don't need to pick up the extension any more. My powers have developed so much I can tell what they're saying through the ceilings and the carpets, and from the rays coming off the telly.

She comes in and gives us a kiss each on top of our heads, just as Beauty is about to do the same to the Beast, and says in a sad-sickly way, 'Have you been in here all along, there's my sweet little girls!' That tight feeling comes in my chest again, and I slip out from under, and say, 'Aw, Mum! It's the good bit, you're spoiling it!'

She says, 'Would you like some chocolate ice-cream as a special treat before bed?'

I feel sort of better and jump off the bed and yell, 'Yeah!'

Though I feel funny, too. Like there's electricity inside me and all the wires about to fuse. I eat so much ice-cream I feel sick.

When Anne's having her bath I go outside and climb up on the shed roof and sit down beside the cat. He looks up and goes stiff.

'Relax,' I whisper, and put my hand on his back. I feel his muscles go soft.

The sick feeling slowly fades.

The cat settles in, but he keeps his eyes wide open, waiting to see what it is I want him for.

It's just starting to stay light at bed time. The blossom above the shed is coming into bud. Over the house there's a

3

white slice moon. I watch it change from flat white to luminous yellow. I can feel my power settling and gathering.

I keep stroking. The power flows from my hand into the cat, making his muscles ripple-twitch.

His eyes turn green.

I open our back door and lead him inside. His feet make soft puffs on the stairs, like faraway fireworks. I let him into my room. He sits quietly as I close my eyes and work a spell.

He says it's over between them, Cass. Oh no, you can tell from his voice that it's the truth. He's utterly wretched. Well, he knows he's been stupid.

Actually no, we've not seen him – he rang from the States. The Philadelphia office wanted him on their Haven Muesli account. It looks like they might want him over there for good.

Well, that's clearly what finished that squalid little affair. It wasn't the kind of thing it would take much to finish – based on a pathetic fantasy as it was. I guess he grabbed the chance to escape. Reading between the lines, she'd started putting on just the kind of emotional pressure he's always tried to avoid. I think he might have learnt his lesson. I think he might be coming to terms at long last with his own emotional needs.

He says he can't wait to see the kids.

The cat curls half-hidden by the heavy white blossom as Dad drives up in his hired car. Dad gets out, we run at him *wham*. He says, 'Hey, steady on!' He lets us lean on him and make him stumble as he goes towards Mum. She's smiling. He puts out his hand and pulls her to him. They put their arms around each other. In the corner of my eye there's an orange flame shooting, and for a moment I think it's my own excitement, leaping out of me, and then I see it's the cat, running along the boundary fence.

Dad gives us: videos, animal pyjama-cases – mine a Colorado bear and Anne's a racoon, a map of Philadelphia to share. Mum smiles and smiles.

He stays three days. On the last day, as he's leaving, Mum says to him; 'Aren't you proud of your girls?' He nods and goes serious and gives us kisses. And then he gets in the car and drives off to Heathrow.

After he's gone Mum comes into my room and says, 'Now what would my wonderful girls like for supper as an extra, extra special treat before bed?'

I don't know why but I scowl and say, 'Oh no, not bed, we wanted to play Beetle!' and my voice comes out whiney, and Anne joins in. Mum looks sort of fed up and panicky.

Then she wrinkles up her nose and asks: 'What on earth's the smell like cat-piss in this room?'

*It just doesn't make sense, Cassie. After it was all so perfect, the whole weekend! I mean, he **agreed**, that we had to sort it out, that it was ridiculous messing around like this, and the sooner we go out and join him the better, now that he's accepted the post in the States.*

I left a message on the ansaphone, the kids sent him a card. Nothing. And now this. He says there's something stopping him. Some kind of block. Well, you know what it is, don't you? It's this whole macho thing. I'd say he was ill. It's a pathology, he's a victim of a social pathology. It's not that he doesn't feel, it's that he feels all too strongly. I mean, all weekend he was bowled over by those kids. And he can't deal with it. A little bit of distance, and he just cuts off again.

I need something to focus the power.

I creep downstairs. Mum's fallen asleep in front of the telly, the college papers she's been marking all around her on the floor. I open the back door. The moon's high and round and covering everything with light like spilt milk.

I don't need to call, I can do it with my mind, and the cat hears with his. He comes. He follows me round the side of the house, sometimes stopping off to watch for mice, then pouring past me and going on ahead. He knows where we're going.

At the rubbish-tip site he sits at the edge while I crunch across the ground. Moonlight nips along the broken glass as I go. I start looking. The cat blinks and waits, flicking his tail. It isn't long before something turns up, the base of a bottle like a bright seeing eye. I dig it out and hold it high. It ripples with moonlight and black fortune-telling shapes.

I look across at the cat. He is watching. He has grown to twice his size.

I place the bottle on my windowsill, right in the middle.

The blossom turns to hard pips of green. Mum takes us to the seaside for the day. As we turn out onto the motorway she sighs. There's a feeling inside the car that makes you hardly able to breathe. Anne is scowling, and suddenly gives me a nasty kick. I kick her back. She screams and punches me. I scream as well. Mum says, 'Stop screaming when I'm driving!' We go on screaming and then Mum says: 'If you don't stop screaming you won't get any crisps!' We scream about that. She cries, 'Stop screaming and you'll get them!' We stop. Anne grins and I grin back, but when Mum throws the crisps to us over her shoulder, they fall on the seat with flat depressing smacks.

At the prom she parks the car. She doesn't move to get out, but sits staring at the sea. We know from this that whatever we ask for now we'll get without even needing to whine or moan. I say, 'Can we go on the donkeys?' and sure enough, in a dull voice she says yes.

Though it's not nice on the donkeys, after all. They waddle and the hairs are rough and rub and hurt your legs and a tired feeling comes up to you through their skin. When we get down Anne goes clingy and grabs hold of Mum's jacket. 'Get off!' says Mum, 'You know how I hate it!' Anne starts crying and clings on harder, swinging out and pulling Mum's jacket wide. Mum gives her a little shove and Anne falls in a deliberate heap on the floor, and Mum has to buy us ice-cream to calm us down.

As we're eating it, Mum says grimly: 'Make the most of it, I might not be able to afford it soon.'

I know what you think, Cass, I know it's unfair of him, leaving me in this state of emotional and financial insecurity. Not knowing what the hell's going on. But I honestly don't think he knows himself. Yes, I know you think I should get myself legal protection, but for a start I don't want to tip him into any wrong decision. And more to the point, I'm not falling into that old trap of making his decisions for him. Helping him hide from his fear of commitment. No, he's got to do it on his own.

Today she sells the car. Now she's got to go to college on the bus, and the next-door neighbour will be taking me and Anne to and from school. I watch from my bedroom window as the man who buys it drives it away. Its movement ripples like vicious snakes in the glass of my bottle.

But there's an orange ripple, too: the cat's tail, reflected, flicking as he sits on my bed.

Even Mum notices what's happened. She comes into my room and sees him and cries, 'Ugh!' He jumps up and darts out, past her, and she shrinks back and shrieks, 'What's that monster doing in here?'

He has grown even bigger. His fangs are longer.

The telephone rings. It's not Cassie, it's Dad. And this time Mum's surprised and excited. She says: 'What? This weekend? What time? You'll be there to meet the kids out of school?'

We come running out of school. They're waiting, together, in the hired car. They're both smiling. I say quickly to Anne: 'Don't ask for an ice-cream,' and she says, just as quickly, 'I wasn't going to'.

We run up, and we can see through the glass that although Dad's trying to be jolly, his grin is like a slit punched in cling-film.

I can feel before she does it that Anne is going to ask for an ice-cream after all, even before we've kissed Dad hello. Mum looks shocked and says in a quick bright panicky voice: 'Of course, my darling, of course!'

Dad looks away, and I have to nudge him for a kiss.

But he said it was all over between them, Cass! Can you believe it? No hint of it before he got here. And then he announces he's taking her *with him back to the States!*

No it was *over, Cass, I'm sure of it, I honestly don't think he had this planned. It's the same old story: he gets over here, he's sucked in by his feelings, he can't cope, he has to put up a barrier. And of course Madam's still waiting in the wings.*

And you should hear it, the rationalization: what he's accusing me of. He dragged up all that stuff about me pressuring him with my maternal desires, I mean, as if it doesn't take two to make a kid. And we had all the usual about me using the kids to tie him down! He says I use them as a weapon, he says it's turned them into monsters. He says, didn't I realize it would drive him away?

We are listening in the kitchen. Greasy pots are stacked everywhere. Cold light wriggles in the puddles on the table.

She puts the phone down and comes through, and seems surprised to find us there.

Anne says instantly, 'I want a lolly from the freezer.'

Mum's eyes are wet, but surprisingly she gets annoyed. She says, 'No'.

Anne stamps her foot.

Mum looks fierce and says in a firm voice we're not used to: 'No!'

Anne's so shocked her mouth falls open and her eyes are like two black dots with surprize. All at once there's a new light feeling in my tummy, making me feel I might rise up off the floor.

Anne recovers. 'Aw, Mum!' she roars.

'No!'

The feeling in my stomach pulls itself together in a tight, neat knot.

Anne knocks her mug off the table and spills her juice on the floor, howling like a dog that someone's kicked.

'Pick it up!' I find myself commanding, as the feeling tightens my legs.

Anne screams.

'Pick it up!' says Mum, though she's starting to yell.

And then she goes all limp and weary, and spoils it all by saying: 'You can only have a lolly if you pick the damn thing up!'

Anne stops crying like a switch pressed and bends to get it and gives me a sly quick grin.

I pull back the curtains and let night into the room. Across the road they've built the foundations. All the treasures we might have saved are buried now for good. I turn to the cat sitting on my bed. He looks up with wide eyes. For a moment I think he's frightened, and I put my hand out to stroke him. He backs. The metal-green sparks in his eyes are scary. His fur stands out on end. He hisses and shows his fangs.

POLISH MUSIC

~

Tessa Hadley

Gail met Jerzy at a concert of Polish folk music at the Arts Centre. There were two kinds of audience there: her kind, dressed in alternative, quirky clothes, interested in 'ethnic' things; and then the mostly elderly, highly respectably turned-out Poles and Ukranians, the men in expensive wool overcoats, the women with silk scarves and grey perms. It was the respectable half of the audience who whupped and slapped their legs and whistled at the music. Gail's friends sat smiling in self-conscious, envious admiration. They were in on something, something 'real'.

Jerzy wasn't Gail's usual type. He had a thick neck, snub nose, small eyes: usually Gail went for small dark men who looked like native Americans. He was sitting next to his father in the row ahead of her, a big man taking up a lot of room, one elbow over the back of the seat next to him, an expanse of hairy wrist and expensive watch showing beyond his striped shirtsleeve, one foot propped up on the other knee. He was doing his share of the shouting and whupping and clapping, enjoying himself.

But at some point that evening – as if all the spirit of the music flashing round the hall suddenly fastened itself in him – Gail was interested in him so that it hurt. She found an excuse to say something to him. When he spoke to women he had a way of drawing himself together courteously without altering how relaxed and comfortable he was. He told her the band was playing at the Polish Club the following night.

She began to drag her friends along to the Polish Club whenever there was music on. There she often saw Jerzy, who came with his father: his wife stayed at home, he scrupulously informed Gail, so that there should be no mistake. 'Nanda thinks it's all too nostalgic, all this folk tradition, harking back to the good old days.' Gail interrogated him about the pictures on the walls: Cardinal Wyszynski, General Sikorski, John Paul II, Mickiewicz, a poet, and some he didn't know. 'I'm not Polish, you know,' he said. 'I'm born here like you. I only keep up all this stuff for the old man's sake.'

He called her the Polish groupie. 'Though why on earth . . .'

'Oh, it's *better*,' she said passionately.

'Better? What's better about it? You should go there.'

'You should meet my parents,' she said. 'Then you'd know. All they ever talk about is deep freezes, lawn-mowers, burglar alarms, the supermarket, the television.'

'Wait until you're grown up,' he said. 'You'll see.'

'They don't have any music in the house. I've never, ever, seen them dance. Some of the women who dance here are my granny's age. Your Dad looks so proud, the way he dresses up with that white scarf, even though he's poorly. My Dad – you know, he gave up. He *wanted* to be middle aged, he sort of waved the white flag, anoraks, slippers . . .'

'My old man's proud alright. But you ought to hear him on social security scroungers. Or on young women with studs through their noses, for that matter, and dyed black hair.'

'But he's always really friendly.' Gail's eyes watered. 'Is that what you think of me?'

'Me?' he said. 'I think you're nuts. But I stick up for you.'

Jerzy gave Gail and her friends a lift home from the Club. They sat politely with their knees together, incongruous in their dishevelled second-hand clothes against the comfortable

beige seats of his three-year-old Volvo. Gail asked him in
for coffee. He looked at her for a moment, his hands heavy
on the steering wheel. 'I think perhaps it's better if I don't,' he
said. 'It's a tempting idea. But I have to get back, I have to be
up for work in the morning.'

But she knew how to find him now, she knew that he ran
his own small business, using chemicals on the outsides of
old buildings. She went down to the docks, where he had a
contract as part of the redevelopment scheme, cleaning the
old Customs House. It was cold, a wind that stank of the low
tide blew off the harbour where the pleasure boats lay sideways on the mud. She wrapped a black scarf around her
head, and was glad of the thick woollen tights she wore
with her Dr. Martens.

He spotted her from where he stood, up on a scaffolding
platform against the building, unrecognizable at a distance
in his yellow waterproofs and helmet. She knew it was him
because when he saw her he stopped his work – he was
directing some sort of high-pressure hose at the bricks – and
stood still, looking at her, for a moment; then he said something to his workmate, handed him the hose, and climbed
down the ladder. He took off his helmet as he came towards
her, rubbed his sweaty, soaking face with a woollen sleeve
from under his waterproofs. His hair was plastered to his
forehead in dark quills.

'I thought I'd come to have a look,' she said.

'Not much to see,' he said. 'But I could make this my break,
if you like. Will you have a coffee?'

He took her into the little white-painted wooden
Norwegian church which had been transplanted to the
waterfront from where the new ring road cut through.
They were the only customers. Gail had the impression that a
cloud of chemical-smelling vapour rose from Jerzy's
waterproofs and filled the little place, steaming the windows.

'Isn't it bad for you, that stuff?' she said.

He had a way of waiting, considering, before he answered her remarks: it was as if she was eccentric and amusing, and couldn't quite be spoken to directly. 'Oh, not if you stand upwind.' Then he added, 'It's only water. What we're using at the moment, on the bricks.'

He watched her make one of her skinny little roll-ups, in black liquorice paper. 'Isn't that bad for you, that stuff?'

'Oh, I *know*, I *know*. One of my friends is a hypnotherapist, she's going to do me some sessions. But I've been smoking since I was thirteen.'

He shook his head slowly, tutting. 'Thirteen! My daughter's age. I wouldn't let her.'

'My Dad didn't know.'

Under the table the weight of his leg came to rest lightly against hers. She was not quite certain at first that it was deliberate, she wondered if he could even feel her through all his layers. Then while they talked she felt the pressure of his leg against hers steadily, deliberately increase, like a humming that rose from imperceptible to filling her ears and all her attention. Still it was one of those invisible things that neither of them need acknowledge. He asked her how old she was and whether she'd been to college, and asked questions about her friends who'd been with her at the Polish Club. When he got up to go she hardly knew if she could stand.

'Shall I take you home?' he said.

Lovemaking with him was different. When she thought back to all the other boyfriends she'd had, it seemed as though in sex with them she had always been so *busy*, working at it, clambering all over them, producing new excitements, even – in one case – getting dressed up in an apparatus, leather and chains and things. But this one didn't require any performance of her. She sometimes wondered if she wasn't boring for him. It wasn't boring for her. Afterwards, he blotted tears from the corners of her eyes with his big blunt fingertips.

Then he showered and dressed, singing – not Polish songs, usually, just snatches of pop songs like anybody would. And she sank down instantly into a deep sleep, before she could even get herself out of bed to wash. He teased her when he kissed her goodbye, before he went back to work. 'Oh, I can sleep anywhere,' she said. 'I always have. Benches in train stations in Europe, with my head on a rucksack. Rolling about in the back of a transit van. I'm famous for it. I could sleep on top of a wall.'

'You know I'm paying my taxes to the government so that you can lie about and sleep!' He stroked her face down to her ears, all one way, as if she was a cat. 'It's me that has to lie awake worrying at night about where the money for the next bill's going to come from.'

'*Do* you lie awake?'

He didn't answer her. 'How you can sleep, in your guilty conscience, in all this filth . . . Didn't you ever learn to pick your clothes up? And in that shower again – it's no use blaming the others – *black* hair . . . Did you contact the landlord? You know it's faulty, the thermostat's gone, someone's going to get hurt. You worry about a few chemicals in your food, but oh, never mind if somebody's scalded to death in your faulty shower!'

'Some hope of the landlord fixing it. How long have we been waiting for the glass in the front window?'

It wasn't just that she left her clothes lying around, picked them up off the floor sometimes and put them back on. Beside his department-store thick cotton shirts, fleece-lined jackets, jeans, her things seemed to be woven out of different elements from a different planet: old crêpe dresses with moth holes in them, frizzled from the launderette; crushed velvet; sometimes, in gaudy parody, crimplene, nylon, net. Her clothes smelled of must and aromatherapy oils; his of fabric softener, ironing. He brought his own shower gel and deodorant, kept them carefully out of the shared bathroom, on a shelf in her room along with his bottle of slivovicza. She sipped his slivovicza sometimes, sometimes he smoked the gear she sprinkled in her liquorice paper roll-ups.

She asked him all about Poland, she wanted him to show her on a map where his family came from. He laughed at her interest and at the same time criticized her because she didn't know any history. She didn't know what had happened in Poland in the war, she had never heard of the Warsaw uprising. She took books on Poland out of the library and tried to read them, she found a collection of Polish folk tales in a second-hand shop. 'I'm born here,' he said. 'I'm not Polish, you know. I only keep it up for my father. I went there once and I didn't like it particularly. For the old folks it's different of course: it's their youth, isn't it?'

But one lunchtime, burying his face against her, he called her *ukochana*.

'What is that,' she asked, 'what did you say?'

'Darling. It means darling. Sweetheart.'

She liked it so much she didn't dare to ask him to say it again, but she waited for it after that, every time.

Vaguely, she and some of the others in the house were in a film maker's co-operative – on the dole, of course. Jerzy was offhandedly intolerant – 'Why don't you ever get anything *done*? What about that idea you had last month, for the dead animals thing? What happened to that?' – but he was always friendly enough when he bumped into any of them. A few times he even drank instant coffee with them all in the front room by the gas fire, sitting on the sagging sofa while Gail curled up on the floor between his knees: he was courteously neutral, almost as if he was a professional come round to mend something and caught short by their alien, suspect hospitality. She thought he even liked Martin, who was modest and musical. Once – they were alone – Gail suggested they make a promotional video for his company. Jerzy laughed incredulously. 'You're not serious? Made by *you lot*? And lose all my business? What were you thinking of, a row of gays in boiler suits kicking up their legs and singing 'Dirt, glorious dirt'?' Actually, that was quite funny – or rather, it was just the sort of thing Terry would have suggested. Sometimes Jerzy surprised her, she thought he actually understood them and how they thought much better than he let on.

Gail had an Aids test. (She had finished with one of the boyfriends – not the one into whips and chains – when she found him and Terry in her bed together. There was still bad feeling between her and Terry. It was the fact that they'd used *her* bed, what was wrong with Terry's own? Terry said she was a possessions-freak.) She was clear. Then she told Jerzy he could stop using anything, that she was having a contraception injection every month because she had been having problems with her periods. (This had been true a couple of years before.) Then she waited. When the time for her period approached, she would visit the lavatory each time with trepidation, hoping not to see blood: when it came she locked the door and sat weeping with her knickers round her ankles – quietly, because she didn't want anyone in the house to know. Finally one month, there was nothing: she made herself wait another week, then she bought one of those do-it-yourself pregnancy testing packs. In excited secrecy, with the armchair pulled across the door to her room, she worked with the little bottles and droppers . . .

When she told Jerzy, at first he was just horribly distressed: something had gone wrong? But when he understood that she had lied to him, he was more angry than she had ever imagined.

'Your ideas and mine, about having a child, bringing up a child, a family . . . Playing at one of your bloody stupid games: don't you understand, a child isn't a game? It's the real thing: for real. You have no idea. Do you think I would let a child of mine grow up in these conditions – in this house – surrounded by this crowd of no-hopers you're mixed up with? In this filth, with drugs and queers and little tarts sleeping around, and the food you eat . . . Can you imagine sterilizing bottles in that kitchen?'

'I won't be sterilizing bottles, I'll be breast-feeding it.'

A snort of derision. 'You'll be doing no such bloody thing.'

'You want me to get rid of it?' she said slowly, incredulously. 'I never, ever thought you'd say that.'

'So what else did you think? That maybe I'd leave my wife and come and live *here*?'

She shook her head. 'We can go on like we are. I can manage. But I never thought you'd consider getting rid of a baby. Being a Catholic.'

'I'm not a Catholic, God Almighty, where do you get this stuff? I haven't been inside a church for twenty-five years.'

She sat on the side of the bed, her hands clenched in a bit of ragged satin patchwork she'd bought in a jumble sale. She remembered the time when her father – utterly improbably, he'd never smacked her once in all her childhood – had said he'd like to take a belt to her. (She'd stayed out all night at a party, her mother had been worried sick.) She had bowed her head in the same stubborn misery, then, hugging her solution to herself. Then, she had left home. Now, she had the baby.

He phoned, four days later: the telephone was in the hall, there was loud music and the noise of voices coming from the front room. Gail crouched and put her finger in her other ear. He had caught her just at the worst time, she was feeling very sick.

His voice was unhappy, loaded. 'How are you?'

'I'm OK.'

'Are you . . . has anything happened?'

'No.'

There was a long pause. 'Alright. I'll come round.'

Then just before he rang off he said, 'You know, you shouldn't drink, you shouldn't smoke, don't you?'

'I'm not.'

'Ah, good girl.'

Once, pushing Cas in his pushchair, Gail saw Jerzy and his wife. It was in an improbable place – improbable for her, anyway: one of those out-of-town DIY superstores. She'd had to push Cas for miles to get there, along the busy out-of-town road in a dirty winter's dusk. But he was wrapped up warmly, and quiet, fascinated by the carousel of passing headlights. Gail was buying a sink unit and a kitchen cupboard. She'd moved out of the shared house (Jerzy had been quite right, it was impossible to bring a baby up there) and into a flat with just a couple of friends, and her mother had given her some money to do something with the kitchen.

Jerzy and his wife were deeply, interestedly pondering the range of ceramic kitchen tiles. Gail stopped quite still at the end of the aisle when she saw them. Calmly she thought, this is my chance to take her in. She was stocky and stout, just as Gail had imagined, but not repulsive: a big humorous mouth, short thick hair with blond highlights.

They didn't look around until Cas called out: Jerzy's name, of course (they hadn't taught him to call Jerzy daddy), but luckily it wasn't clear, the woman couldn't possibly have known. Gail pushed the pushchair towards them with a blank face, pretending to be interested in the anaglypta wallpapers. She stopped near them, fingering textures.

'Oh look, Jerry, he likes you.' The woman smiled at Cas, bent down, tickled his knee. 'What a handsome chap, *aren't* you?' Cas favoured her with a quick smile, reached up his arms to be picked up by Jerzy. 'They always like the men, don't they? My two were just the same. Take us women for granted.'

'That's right,' Gail agreed, blushing, bending over Cas, worrying that he would wriggle out of his straps now and insist on being picked up. 'He loves men.'

'What's his name?'

She hadn't thought of that. There was a flash – not of the eyes, they hadn't yet looked at one another – between her and Jerzy. 'Oh, Charles. Chas. After his father.'

'That's nice,' said the woman. 'I like the old-fashioned names.'

Jerzy disappeared round a corner. 'Come and have a look at these,' he called to his wife.

'OK,' she said reluctantly, her eyes returning absorbedly to the tiles she liked, estimating and imagining. 'But I really think these are the ones I want.'

Cas let out a roar of disappointment, and Gail had to undo his straps and lift him out of his chair.

Fifteen minutes later Jerzy found her in the kitchen department. She was letting Cas crawl around in a mock kitchen while she worked out what she could afford, keeping an eye on him, making sure he didn't pull anything over on himself, stick his fingers in any electric sockets. This was all taking up so much of her attention that she wasn't even thinking consciously about her encounter.

Jerzy picked Cas up, nuzzled him, buried his face in his tummy, tickling, made Cas squeal with delight. 'She's gone in the one next door. She thinks I'm in the car park. What are you doing bringing him out here in all this weather? Did you *walk*?'

Gail looked hard at him. 'Give us a lift then.'

He didn't answer: it made him look at the baby in that way he had, tenderly baffled, brooding.

'Your wife isn't Polish,' Gail said to him suddenly.

'Polish? Whoever said she was? Of course she isn't Polish!'

'But I always thought . . . I don't know. I just picked it up from somewhere . . . the name or something . . .'

'Nanda? But Nanda isn't a Polish name. Fernanda: although she never tells anyone. After some great aunt or something.'

'It *sounded* . . . But she was just ordinary. Well, not ordinary. Just like anyone.'

On their way home it began to snow. It was dark: in the cones of orange light under the street lamps and in the headlight beams, the flakes swam, weightless and leisurely. The cars slowed slightly, their windscreen wipers worked, the roar of the three lane highway was muffled. Gail wrapped her wool scarf round her head. Cas was tightly tucked in: the flakes were landing on his coat and his blanket but she didn't pull his plastic covers down because she didn't want him to miss it, his first snow.

'Look, Cas, snow. Isn't it lovely?'

His eyes were huge under his woolly hat, drinking it in. Gail was happy. She hummed a tune from one of her tapes of Polish folk music whose words she would never understand. She and Cas were making their way through a forest of dark pines, the first snow settling along their branches, a round white moon hanging overhead, the thin crust of snow crunching on the carpet of pine needles underfoot. At the same time she was pleased with her new kitchen cabinets, and watchful of the cars throwing up their wake of slush as they passed; she stopped at traffic lights, waiting for the green man to signal them across. After all Jerzy's wife had only been like anybody else. She felt for the first time that it was *hers*, this magic: the moon and the snow and the secret silence of the forest.

THE FOREST

~

Christine Harrison

The smell of resin in the forest was strong, like the smell of the sea. And, as the salty sea smell clings to the clothes of sailors, so the pungent smell of resin clung to the clothes of the foresters. Their shirts and trousers were stained with it. Their hands were stained with it. And it ran down the bark of the felled trees.

To Barbara the forest was like a home, and its moist smells nourished and comforted her. The trees made a roof over her head, a dark sheltering roof.

Every school day she had to cycle through the forest, keeping to the narrow path thick with several years' fall of pine needles, softly bumping over tree roots and occasional stones. As it happened, in truth, it was the best thing in her life, this ride through the forest to and from school. She came out of her dream. For the rest of her life seemed shadowy, as if lived by someone she hardly knew. It was only in the forest that she felt fully alive. As if it was her real home.

The foresters themselves, Polish nearly all of them, lived in caravans in clearings in the forest, and even in converted horse boxes. Living mostly without women, they worked hard, getting quietly drunk at weekends. On Sundays a lorry-load of them with hangovers went to Mass in Taunton. They worked throughout the daylight hours, sleeping rough, drinking their sweet black tea which they brewed on little fires that glowed in the dark forest. A few of them though did have women, wives or common-law wives, and there was a handful of children – these were the children that Barbara taught. One or two of the women helped with the work in the forest, trimming the smaller branches from the trees and peeling the bark with a sharp tool. One or two women had young babies, and lived isolated and uneventful lives, their men at work all day long.

Every day, on her way to school, Barbara passed one of these women. This was Lily.

Usually Lily was looking out over the half-door of her converted horsebox. She was married to one of the Polish foresters, and had a baby of about six months. Barbara thought she was probably a local woman, her accent seemed local – though it was hard to tell as she spoke very little, and in monosyllables.

Lily was thought to be simple. It was a word that did not quite convey her half-baked complexity. Simple perhaps in her needs – these were scarcely human in their restricted simplicity. There was something amoebic, anchorite, in the way she never left the horsebox and the little patch of cleared forest round it. Lily's complexity lay in the depths of her obscure, unknowable personality, layer on layer, clear on top, murky and unset and raw underneath.

The horsebox was very compact, like a ship's cabin. Everything had a place. During the day the baby's wooden rocker was stowed gipsy-style under the marriage bed with its thin hard mattress. On one wall there was a glass-fronted china cupboard hanging on two huge nails. Lily had beautified the shelves of this cupboard with empty silver foil cases from shop-bought jam tarts and she had spaced out the three chipped and stained tin mugs, nicely laying them on lacy paper doilies. A red enamel kettle for tea and a large kettle for hot water for washing were permanently on the boil on the stove. The stove was the heart and life of this home. Lily had her washing line tied between two trees, but the dripping and moisture from the trees seldom allowed anything to dry properly and she had to string the half-dried things above the hot little stove, where they sometimes scorched. The place smelled of scorched flannel, babies – and resin.

Barbara always waved, and called out something cheerful, 'It's going to clear up later I think', or 'Lovely morning to put the baby out', and Lily would sometimes wave – but sometimes look as if she had not heard or did not want to hear. She might be simple, thought Barbara, but she's temperamental. She regarded the woman's life with horror, terror almost. It was not that Barbara did not love the forest. But to be trapped in it?

On her ride back from school Barbara would pass Lily again. The baby would usually be having its afternoon nap. This was the time when Lily got out her book. It was an ancient Girls' Annual. Lily looked at the pictures of gym-slipped girls with lacrosse sticks and she ate jam tarts that she bought from the travelling van.

Once or twice Barbara had got off her bicycle and tried to start a conversation, but was met with suspicion.

Barbara did not realise that Lily suspected every woman her husband might lay eyes on, though these were few enough. She waited all day for him to come home to her, passing her day looking out over the half-door, her baby on her arm, hauling the water from a rain butt to wash the baby's clothes, or getting the stove to burn. All day she kept her hair in rags to curl it, taking them out before she polished the red kettle and set out two enamel plates, two knives and two spoons ready for the evening meal.

When he did come home at dusk, Lily would watch him while he washed, his hands and body still streaked with the strong-smelling resin. As he washed his naked body, the rivulets of resin which ran down his arms would not wash off. At night he would lie beside her in the fug of the horse-box – she, enveloped in the folds of her huge flannel nightdress (for she was prudish in her primitive way) which was rough with fierce washings and warm and scorched with drying over the stove. The baby slept in its rocker beside them.

At night the voices of wood pigeons and owls came from the forest.

Barbara sometimes wondered what it was like at night in the forest. She rented two rooms in the village pub. Cool dark rooms. Her bed by the window allowed her to see the night sky.

On the windowsill Barbara put things she had brought home from the forest – fir cones, a few wood anemones.

In the evening she sat preparing her lessons for the next day.

If they were busy downstairs, she would help out in the bar. Sometimes two or three of the Polish foresters would come in for a drink, but they were always well behaved and quiet and never had more than one drink during the week. She had a peaceful, ordered life, her supper brought up on a tray by the publican's wife. Emotionally it was a solitary existence. The best thing, the thing she looked forward to, was the ride through the forest in the mornings, and then after school, the ride back. Then she felt inside her skin as at no other time or place.

As she cycled steadily on her way back and forth to school she heard, as well as the soft bumping of the wheels of the machine, the whine of the rapacious chainsaws. It was the foresters who worked felling, stripping and stacking the fir trees – they worked piece work, and so they worked fast and hard, in a regular rhythm, never stopping for long. From time to time Barbara passed one or two at work by the path-side. Sometimes they looked up, sometimes they laughed and said something to each other in their own language. If she said good morning they would smile back with bold shy smiles, their reticence overlaid with a certain male swagger. But they scarcely paused in their work. Occasionally she passed a man who preferred to work alone. Felling a tree alone is very skilled. As it crashes down with an accelerating speed, bringing with it a shipwreck of broken branches and twigs, it could kill a man.

An ex-army hut had been hauled through the main forest road and set up on the edge of the forest to use as a schoolroom. Altogether there were about a dozen children between the ages of four and ten, after that they had to go to school in the town. Half of them spoke no English, and Barbara had only a few words of Polish. She managed with sign language and smiles. If they had not been a quiet docile lot she could not have managed. Only one or two spoke good English.

She taught them to read. She taught them little songs. Sometimes they painted pictures of the forest and their fathers wielding huge chainsaws, their mothers stripping the smaller branches from the fallen trees. The older ones frowned over mathematics books, while the little ones threaded beads and wound them round their brown wrists like bracelets.

At lunchtime they brought out their packed lunches and then they would chat to each other in their native language and eat little shrivelled apples and heavy home-made cake.

At the end of the afternoon school, their mothers came to fetch them, strong women in wellington boots staring in at the window.

Barbara locked up the schoolroom and packed her books into the satchel on the back of her bicycle.

She usually took more or less the same way back through the forest, though sometimes she chose a slightly different path which met up later with her usual homeward way. Once or twice she had become briefly lost for a while. She was not really lost this warm May afternoon. Not lost. But she had wandered off her most direct path. She did not want to get to the village too quickly. It was lovely in the forest, quite magical, the sun slipping through the leaves of fir, beech and oak which grew on the periphery of the main fir forest, whose heart was thuya and sitka. Beams of sunlight streamed through the leaves and branches, silky bright as from some angelic source.

Barbara got off her bicycle and pushed it over the knotty tree roots on the little narrowing path.

In the distance she could hear the frantic whine of the chainsaws rising and falling.

She was so sure she was alone in that part of the forest that the sight of a man standing quite still there beside a tree frightened her. She had thought at first he *was* a tree and then that he was an animal of some kind. She recognized then who it was. It was Lily's husband, a thickset man of about forty, with a dark drooping moustache. Lily's husband.

He just stood there, as the sun flickered leaf patterns over his face and body.

She remounted and rode slowly on, nearer and nearer to him. He stepped towards her and took hold of the handle-bars, nearly making her fall. But she was not frightened at all now. It was just Lily's husband. She dismounted.

'You have come the wrong way,' he said, in good English.

'You are Lily's husband,' she said. He did not answer. Then he said, 'I will show you another way'.

'I can find my own way.' Her words rang out between the trees.

'I will show you,' he said, pretending not to understand her rejection. Still holding the bicycle by the handlebars he set off into the wood. He walked quickly, not looking back, and if she had not followed him he would soon have been lost in the trees. She could think of nothing else to do but follow him.

After a while he stopped though, and let her catch up with him.

She stood there beside him waiting for him to relinquish her bicycle. He held on to it, saying nothing, looking at her with a curious expression, both shy and as if he was nearly laughing at her, looking at her yellow full skirt, her soft white sweater, her bare legs and old brown laced-up shoes. She felt transfixed by his gaze, and at the same time she was experiencing a horrible crawling sensation in her flesh. She was revolted by him in some peculiar way as she might have been if her own father had made some forbidden approach. She did not understand this. She was aware of his maleness. She could not avoid it, sidestep it. She thought of him in this context in a strange way. He is a used-up male, she thought at the back of her mind, dimly, father of a child, another woman's husband; sex to him is an everyday thing, a habit. To her it was not, it was delicate and new, hardly tried. These thoughts of hers did not form words in her mind.

She started to become angry with him, that he would not hand over her bicycle, and immediately he sensed this, and with a small laugh, handed it to her. He pointed out the path she should take, and she felt him watch as she got on the bicycle and unsteadily rode off.

After she had ridden for a while, she came to the clearing which was Lily's forest home.

Lily was putting curling rags into her brown hair, which was all different lengths. She was doing this expertly, with quick fingers, without using a mirror.

She looked at Barbara, who at once thought the woman somehow knew what had happened. But that must be imagination, as it was impossible. And anyway there was nothing to know.

'It's a lovely afternoon. Is the baby asleep?' she said.

'Yes,' said Lily. She twisted another rag into her hair.

Barbara decided she would not think any more about it. She put it right out of her mind.

And she did not see Lily's husband for several weeks. She had forgotten all about him.

Then, one day, there he was in her classroom. He had actually come into her classroom, just walked in. She had been drawing a star shape on the blackboard, she was colouring it in with yellow chalk, writing its name beside it for the children to copy. A star.

Suddenly he was there, standing beside her, and the children had gone very quiet. They weren't used to seeing a man there, except once a week when the vicar came in his robes and smiled strangely at them. This man was out of place in the classroom. He might have sprung from one of the story books, a giant streaked with resin.

'I have come to ask for something,' he said. It was as if the children were invisible to him, he was not aware of them. He spoke only to her.

Barbara did not reply. Her tongue had frozen in her mouth. She was as if stunned, unbelieving, her thoughts stilled inside her head. That he should come into the classroom like this. None of the other men, not one would have done this. The classroom was an alien place to them, territory that would never be broached even if they had a child in the school. Even the mothers did not seem to want to come further than the door. It was the way it was. He began searching for words. He came very close to her.

'Will you teach Lily to read,' he said.

'Lily,' she said faintly whispering.

'Will you say yes,' he asked. He insisted.

She was overwhelmed by him. She agreed without thinking. She wanted him to go.

And so, after that, on her way home from school, all through that summer she stopped at the horsebox that was Lily's home and began to try to teach Lily to read.

She made cards which said 'baby' and 'jam tarts' and 'book' and all the things she thought Lily was interested in. She taught Lily the sounds of the letters and how to write her husband's name – Oscar – she already knew how to write her own name, but that was all. She tried to teach her how to build up words, and also how to recognize word patterns, in case she found that easier.

She would call in and have a cup of tea with sterilized milk and teach Lily how to read 'tree, baby, milk, apple, bird'. Lily copied the words, her tongue between her teeth. Lily wanted to read her book about the girls who played lacrosse. She was not very interested in the book Barbara tried to teach her from, about two small children called Dick and Dora.

She made very slow progress, if any at all. She wanted to learn, but could not retain anything in her head from one day to the next. Barbara began to feel that her task was impossible. Lily was indeed very simple. And although Barbara had now spent many hours with her, she knew as little about the woman herself as she had at the beginning. It was as if it would have needed something different from words to communicate with her. She began to think she was wasting her time trying to teach her to read, and began to lose heart. She did not know if Lily was losing heart.

One day Lily's husband came home early from work. It had never happened before, wasting daylight when he could be earning money. Lily still had her hair in curlers and was overcome with embarrassment. She went to the darkness at the back of the horsebox, and bending her head away from him started to pull the rags from her hair.

'Can Lily read yet?' he asked Barbara.

Barbara could not bring herself to tell him that his wife probably would not be able to learn to read. That she was too – simple.

'She is not learning very fast,' she said.

'It will take time,' said the Pole.

The baby woke up, hearing its father's deep voice, and began to cry. The man picked the child out of his little wooden bed, and began tenderly speaking in Polish to it. Then, with an encouraging nod of his head, as if to brook no refusal, he gave the baby to Barbara to hold.

As she held Lily's baby, Barbara felt fear and disgust at the smell of its wet nappy and the sight of milky saliva dribbling from its gummy mouth. It stopped crying and gave her a toothless smile, but she was not won over, only now felt guilt at the hardness of her heart.

Nevertheless something had moved within her. It had to do with the feeling she had as she cycled home through the forest. But less pleasant, more disturbing and new and imprisoning. Now she knew why the forest smelled salty and milky. It had to do with this warm baby in her arms.

She felt disgusted by it all. Everything. The cramped little place where they were all squashed in. The warmth of the stove on this fine evening. The Pole's hairy arms, stained with resin, as he washed his hands in the tin basin, the pathetic doilies and jam tart cases on the shelves. Everything.

'I must go,' she said.

'Have some tea,' said the Pole, drying his hands on a nappy he had taken from the line over the stove.

'I must go,' she said, handing the baby to its mother, 'I'm sorry, I must go.'

'Come again. For another lesson.'

She looked at him helplessly, not knowing what to say.

'It will take time,' he said.

ROUGH BOYS

~

Jenny Sullivan

Raucous, crow-coarse voices: jeering, jostling, cat-calling, the Rough Boys swaggered into our wood swiping with sticks, kicking leaves, hurling stones, arrogant princes taking loud possession of their birthright.

We dared not approach them. We feared their mockery, their differentness. Thin white legs with bony feet thrust into laceless, holed black daps, snake belts cinching cut-down grey trousers and fraying pullovers over bareskin ribs made us embarrassed by our petticoats, gingham and prissy socks. My cousin Maggie and I followed from a distance, carefully avoiding their eyes, but they were as aware of us as we were of them, although we never spoke. Especially not me. Maggie's Mam was a paper millgirl, her fingertips cross-hatched with blackened papercuts, her shins flowering with purple bruises from the great, circular reels of uncut paper. She spoke the language of the workplace, scattered with dropped aitches, bristling with profanities. My own mother laboured at home, thigh deep in kids, her company the radio. She, too, spoke the language of her workplace, BBC English, and her children, by God, would do likewise.

The first time I dropped an aitch, she had me enrolled with Miss De Lacey, Elocutionist, before it hit the floor. Saturday mornings I wrestled vowels into submission and snapped terminal 't's' like spit on a hot iron until my aitches were harnessed, and my vowels fell like ripe Victoria plums.

'Listen and imitate, child!' haunted my dreams. 'Listen and

imitate, imitate' – and feel by-the-way the rhythmic roll and toss of poetry, the graceful curve of rhyme, the shiver and tingle of perfect words. Imitate – and ride with Lochinvar out of the West; anguish with the Highwayman; knock on the moonlit door.

I trod carpets of thin anemones, heard the otter whistle, recognized each turn in the old, lost road through the woods. I knew it well, that wood; summers with Maggie. One week each year, I was despatched to the bus-stop with a slap on the backside and the instruction to 'Behave yourself for Aunty – and be sure you stay right away from rough boys, d'you hear?' My mother knew I was venturing into wild, uncharted, alien country infested with dangerous males.

Maggie lived in a grey pebbledash council semi, her running space grey streets linked by a warren of gwlis; her house had a 'back' instead of a garden, and wire and concrete fences instead of neat boundary walls and clipped hedges. Up the hill, the freedom of the summer woods went on forever.

Maggie was ten, like me, and seventeen-year-old Di was detailed to mind us while their parents worked. Promising terrible vengeance if we split, as my aunt pedalled down the road and my uncle's works van sputtered away, Di was gone, slipping under the wire of the back fence and into the gwli. And we were free.

We queened all day in the sunlit woods, wading through cool bluebell lakes under a brilliant sky, wild garlic woven into bridal crowns for our tangled, mousy hair. Clear sap from blue spears, wrenched white-rooted from the earth, dripped on our gingham dresses and made snail trails on bare legs. Conservation hadn't been invented, then. The bluebells would be back next year, they always came, like summer itself.

'Make up a story with us in it, kidder,' Maggie begged, and I filled our wood with princes, wizards, elves. I harnessed unicorns, their silvery hooves and horns gleaming in the shafts of sunlight filtering through the branches above our heads, and together we rode the snowy beasts up into the arched green. We flew madly and joyfully like birds, spiralling between bluebells and sky. If there had been a rainbow, there would have been a pot of gold at each end. But there were never rainbows, because it never rained, and we rarely saw an adult from woods' edge to woods' end. Then, rakish and piratical, came the Rough Boys, and captured us.

The dark brown river ran ominously through the woods, roiling like the submerged coils of a snake in the centre deeps, sluicing clear and cold at its muddy, gravelled edge. The boys, shouting and splashing, dared it first, we slipping in a few timid yards away, socks stuffed into sandals clutched firmly in our hands, skirts tucked into knicker-legs, flinching and biting our lips at the cold sting of the water. Silvery bodkin tiddlers and blunt bullheads stitched in and out of the dark weed trailing like drowned hair in the shallows.

The remains of a bridge spanned the river, sinister black iron, the two sides arcing across, although you had to clamber up onto the first piling, where it had parted from the bank, to reach it. The wooden walkway had long since rotted through and fallen, and the only way to cross was to cling on to the top girder and walk crabwise along the narrow ledge at the bottom, nose pressed prayerfully to hexagonal metal bolts. We watched the boys cross, one after another, fearless, purposeful black ants, our breaths caught and held until each one leapt safe and loud with relief onto the opposite bank. We knew the tale of the boy who fell from the bridge – broke his back, of course, and drownded in agony before he could be fished out. Late at night, they said, you could hear his screams, echoing over the sinister river . . .

I wanted to be on the other side with the rough boys: to kick over the traces, to misbehave, be a rough girl, even if it meant drownding horribly, broken-backed, in the tearaway river. Maggie pleaded with me, *no don't*, gnawing her knuckles, but I was scrabbling, scrambling up the piling, climbing on the black bridge, breathing the musky heat of the day soaked into the girder, rust-bubbles popping under my white-knuckled fingers, my toes snatching like claws at the narrow ledge. Before I reached the other side, Maggie was crossing too, pausing where the curve-backed river was deepest, her face clenched like a fist, gathering courage.

The Rough Boys had made a den, and we were allowed inside, because we had crossed the river. 'Orright for girls, considrin'', they said, beating us on the back with their bony, dirty, Rough Boy hands. Torn down branches draped across a mossy, fallen trunk made a roof and walls, and Maggie and me crowded with them into their leaf-mould smelling haven, their scabby, dirty knees wedged against our white legs.

Fervent, fascinated acolytes, we watched them shred discarded dog-ends and roll brown-stained emaciated cigarettes in a Rizla machine stolen from the corner shop. They smoked the tarry sticks with care and ceremony and after, vomited neatly, quietly, like cats. We drank cold tea from a passed-round pop bottle, ate jam sandwiches and sour, scrumped apples, and stuck our licked fingers into a communal bag of sherbet, dyeing our fingers yellow as the gaudy sun. Maggie talked broad-voiced as them, loud, raucous, coarse, her ready cursing a schooldays camouflage. But I was silent, not afraid of the Rough Boys but knowing that schooled vowels and brittle terminal consonants would end all this, lose their fragile trust, set me 'posh' and 'snooty' and apart from this magical, alien, forbidden company. I dared not speak.

The biggest boy, piebald neck revealing the infrequent passage of soap, undid his snake belt and his trouser buttons, producing his insignificant pride. He waggled it carefully, thoughtfully, like a captured worm, and Maggie obligingly screamed, but I was made of sterner stuff. I had brothers, and such miserable appendages held no mystery. Before I could stop myself:

'Ey, kid,' I hollered, 'jew wanna borrow a pin fer yer li'l winkle?'

'Imitate my cadences, child, listen to my speech.' Miss De Lacey's lessons had taken root. But not as she intended: I spoke their language, not hers.

My words brought derisive, traitorous hoots of pleasure from the other boys: his face flamed scarlet with shame.

Willie Flash he became. Willie Flash shared stolen beer with us, and stripped to ragged grey underpants to catch tiddlers, which we tried to cook over a smoky fire. He brought stolen sweets and wonderful balloons which inflated to amazing lengths when blown into, and came each in its own neat foil packet. I climbed trees in bare feet and knickers, cursed, blasphemed, made my voice grating, loud, raucous as a rook: I was a Rough Girl.

We had the Rough Boys one week, one summer, and on the very last day, Willie Flash took a dark holly leaf, and with surgical concentration punctured seven flinching thumbs while we hissed spit through gritted teeth. We mingled squeezed red and grime: blood-siblings forever. Rough boys, rude boys, thin, dirty, wild, wolfish boys, our friendship sealed in scarlet, and memories rising with a bluebell tide creeping at the edge of a wood, early summer, brightness and a swift brown river.

Then, we lost our woods. Maggie forsook them after I left, and next year we were looking for tidier, older, respectable boys, and thinking about kissing. Summer ended, and I went home.

I went home, dumping my luggage on the kitchen floor. My mother scraped brown curls from a potato into the sink.

'Hello, Mummy. Something smells good,' I said, my structured vowels smooth and innocuous as eggs, my t's sharp as spit. 'What is there for tea?'

My mother smiled, content.

There had been no Rough Boys.

MISTAKEN IDENTITY

~

Jo Hughes

Committee rooms. Committee rooms that are big and blank and impersonal. With tables arranged in a square, circle or rectangle. Chairs with leather seats all placed just so. All facing inwards. All facing each other. Each placed one foot from its neighbour. Twelve inches, very precise.

This is where the world turns. Men and women in suits sit here. They say yes, no, nod sagely. They make amendments, think, talk, jot notes. The walls that surround them are white and bare except for one large portrait which watches them. A man in a suit done in oils. How did he find the time in his busy schedule to pose? Did his wife suggest the green serge suit? Or was it debated on by the committee? And the tie? That's surely the old school tie? Or the Honourable Member's tie? None but the initiated will recognize it. For them it marks him. Points to his importance in the world.

Every time the cleaner comes into this room she bows to the picture. She does this because she can. Because no one is looking. Because no one would care. For her it's become like touching wood to stop bad things from happening. Like throwing spilt salt over her left shoulder to blind the devil. And besides that he looks a bit lonely up there on the wall. His eyes, she thinks, look sad.

The cleaner is eighteen years old and has long blonde pony-tailed hair and a pretty face. She wears jeans, trainers, an old sweater that belonged to her brother and a shapeless overall of baby-blue nylon which she hates. Everyone recognizes the overall. It marks her out. Shows her place, just as the man's suit shows his. But the cleaner doesn't make the world turn, she just cleans it.

She squirts the world with polish, rubs it with a cloth until it shines. Removes its ashtrays and empty coffee cups, vacuums it, empties its waste-paper bins. Places its chairs in their regimented positions, twelve inches between each. One foot. Just so. She doesn't water the plants, that's someone else's job. She doesn't rearrange the tables. Doesn't open or close the blinds. Doesn't touch the picture, except to carefully run the feather duster across the frame. Of the last, she is certain she is doing right, as the supervisor was clear on that point. 'Don't polish this,' she had said, 'and don't scrub it with Vim either.' As if. How stupid did the woman think she was?

When the cleaner comes here at night, after all the committee members and the managers and personal assistants and secretaries and word processors and receptionists have gone home, the room is hers. She wheels her trolley up the corridor, unloads the vacuum, the cans of polish, the dusters and the black plastic bags, then carries it all into the committee room and lays it out in readiness. Sometimes the room looks just the same as when she left it the day before. It looks just as if no one had been in there at all. She peeps in the waste-paper bin nearest the door. It's empty. Not even an illicit cigarette-end or a suspect tissue, and she's seen plenty of both. So the room is spotlessly clean. That would please her if she could knock off early, but she can't and so she glances at her watch in order to judge how much time she has to kill.

Instead of vacuuming the floor she runs her eye over it. She finds one tiny fleck of lint, probably from her duster last night, and picks it up between thumb and forefinger and drops it in her rubbish sack. Next she decides to polish the table. This is partly so that the room will smell freshly-cleaned, but mostly because she actually enjoys doing this. Sometimes, when she is in a particularly indignant mood, she sprays words in large letters across the table. Words like 'WANKERS' or 'ARSEHOLE'. Today she's in a gentler frame of mind so she sprays a large heart and inside it writes 'Olivia loves . . .' She hesitates then – who does she love? – and settles for a question mark.

Olivia. What a name to be stuck with. She blames Olivia de Havilland for this indignity. Olivia de Havilland, Gone With The bloody Wind and her mother's over-romantic imagin-ation. She gets her duster and draws it over her words in large sweeps, turns her love into a beautiful shine. A shine that will reflect the faces of the committee members. A shine which will mirror their eloquent frowns, their expensive shirts. Their ties will make a river of colour with their stripes of blue and emerald and scarlet and gold. As if they'll notice. But it passes the time. Offers a little variation, a stand against the tedium.

Olivia does corridor 'Q' which consists of one committee room, five offices, two public toilets, male and female, and two private 'washrooms', also male and female. She does the corridor itself which is the most boring part, being straight and long. The equivalent, she thinks, of motorways for long distance lorry drivers. This work takes three hours out of her life each evening from Monday to Friday. On Saturday she works in the market selling bread, a job she's had since she was fifteen. On Friday and Saturday night she works in the Quayside Nitespot as a barmaid. Olivia's friend Sue works in the casino and says she'll try to get Olivia work there. The pay's not much better but the tips are good. 'Oh,' says Sue, 'the tips. You wouldn't believe it.' Olivia does believe it, but all she can do is wait and hope . . .

Olivia's been cleaning corridor 'Q' since she started this job back in June. It's now the beginning of December and she no longer wonders what the rest of the building is like. She no longer yearns to see corridors A, B, C, D, E, F, G, H, I, J, K, L, M, N, O and P – leave alone clean them. All she wants to do now is get a better job. Get a better job and fall in love.

More than any other, the big committee room with its floor-to-ceiling windows and its starkness makes her aware of the changes in the weather and the seasons. In June she watched the sun sink while she cleaned the room and went home in the last of its light. Now it's dark when she arrives and the windows, with only blackness behind them, have become enormous mirrors. Out there, beyond the brightly-lit room, another room hovers like a twin world. The cleaner can see herself, a little figure in a blue overall. A nobody. It reminds her of that poem about nobody which the teacher had read aloud at school. It had been the first time she'd been touched by words in the alien language of poetry. She remembered how she'd felt a sweet lilt of recognition in the pit of her stomach, and breathed an involuntary sigh, and then Ed Thomas had said, in his belligerent, full-of-it way, 'Yeah, but she's not nobody, is she, Miss? She wouldn't be in the book if she was no one.' The teacher – one of those new young hopeful ones – had just wilted into silence, while Ed Thomas had given the class an evil leer and rocked his chair back, his arms resolutely folded, proud to be an angry zero who could see through all the lies.

This December the weather is mild, but in the office black heat blasts from the radiators regardless. Olivia's feeling uncomfortably hot. She hasn't been sitting still, coolly talking, calmly shuffling paper, she's been pushing around an industrial-size vacuum. She's been rubbing and lifting and shifting and lugging and scrubbing, and she's hot.

The overall is sticky so she unzips it and takes off her jumper. She takes off her shoes and socks, hopping about to keep her balance. She was going to keep the overall on over her T-shirt, but that's even more uncomfortable. The clammy nylon sticks to the skin of her arms and neck, so she throws the hated garment through the door where it lands near her trolley. Now that she's just in her jeans and T-shirt she feels much better. Not only cooler but also much more herself.

She checks her watch. There's still time to kill. She goes to the corner of the room and stands, back erect, head and arms held high as if she were about to dive into a pool. She's aware of the carpet hot and bristling under her feet. Of her breathing and her stillness. Then she throws the top part of her body down and forward. Her hands reach the floor and her legs arc upward and for a moment she hovers there like an acrobatic toy. Then she flips down into a crab, but she can't quite lift herself into the standing position again, so she collapses instead. Next she throws herself into four perfect cartwheels, one after another, which bring her to within inches of the window.

Momentarily dizzy, Olivia faces her reflection, remembers that this glass is not a mirror, but a window, imagines reports of gymnastic goings on. Imagines the supervisor's sarcasm, her own humiliation. She frowns, then cups her hands around her eyes and presses her brow on the cold glass and stares out. The town is spelled out in a constellation of street lights. Over the far hills patterns of yellow dots traverse the night. Nearby four towers of bright white light illuminate the football ground and closer still, across the car park and the dual carriageway, the prison offers its broken rectangles of half-light to the stars, to her eyes.

Unlike the little terraced houses with their downstairs glow and flicker of blue TV, and unlike the flats with their patterns of occupation and emptiness, the prison has only two states. There, all the cell lights are uniformly either off or on, regardless of the occupants' needs or desires. Olivia stares at the curtainless windows and wonders who lives beyond them, what men they imprison. She doesn't imagine rapists or murderers. She knows that they are there, but thinks instead about the beaten men, the half-innocent, the young, gone-wrong, never-given-a-chance men. Men like her brother Jake. But Jake is in Strangeways in Manchester. If he was here she'd be able to visit him. She'd be able, maybe, to wave to him.

She counts the windows. There are ten across by five down. Fifty windows. Fifty souls. Fifty narrow beds. She imagines a man like Jake. He's probably in there for drugs, like Jake. Probably only sold stuff to his friends. Then found he suddenly had a lot of friends, like Jake. Then no friends, also like Jake. She'd been to see Jake once since he'd been inside. The journey took four and a half hours and someone on the train, an insipid woman in a pink shell suit with three screaming children, had sat with her and attempted a conversation. 'Visiting friends?' she'd said. Olivia had just said 'No,' and turned away.

Olivia looks away from the main block of old grey stone to the newer red brick extension and counts the windows again. Eight across and only three down. And then she sees him.

He's standing on the second floor at the third window from the left. His arms are outstretched, holding the bars at shoulder level. She can't see his face, the light behind him makes him a silhouette. But she can read his sadness in that pose. He's a crucifixion of misery. He doesn't move.

Does he see her?

Tentatively, she raises one arm and makes a slow arc at the night.

And slowly, like a strange mirror which responds only after a mis-timed delay, like a star whose light reaches earth long after its last flicker has died and given way to endless night, the figure raises its arm in an echoing arc.

In the prison, the guard, who has been standing by the window in the staff room, yawns and, as is his habit, fingers the heavy metallic bulk of the keys that hang from his belt. He smiles as he thinks of the girl in the office block opposite.

The night hangs between them, a curtain of blackness. Far away and long ago, unnoticed by either of them, a nameless star gives its last violent pulse of light, shrinks down to the volume of zero and becomes a black hole that swallows everything within its pull.

A WILD BOY

~

Christine Harrison

Dorothy was picking peas in the garden when the news was brought to her. She looked up and saw her neighbour Harry Wilkins's face. It looked all fallen away. He shut the gate carefully and led her inside the house. From then on it was as if a ceremony had been laid on her ordinary life, like a heavy, deep-dyed tapestry cloth. Harry asked her to sit down. 'I have something to tell you, Dorothy. I am very sorry.' Dorothy sat down, not in her usual armchair but on one of the straight-backed chairs with rush seats against the wall. She knew before she was told what had happened. Billy was dead.

After she had been given this news Dorothy came out of her cool dark little cottage, back into the garden. She went on with her task of picking the peas. The green pods, hanging amongst green leaves and tendrils and an occasional white flower, were hard to see. She picked carefully, slowly, not breaking down the fragile plant. After a while Harry Wilkins came out of the house and stood watching her. 'His neck was broken,' he said. 'There was never any pain.' He began helping her to pick the peas. 'They took him to the Queen Mary's.' The basket was full and Dorothy handed it to him. 'Have them for your dinner,' she said, and then, 'You'd better take me there.' She went with him to the car.

She had a sprig of mint in her fingers and she pinched it sometimes and sniffed it. This scent was now part of the ceremony. Later she watched herself identifying her son's body.

That night she breathed in the sweet summer air as she lay in bed. It was a warm night. The sky was full of stars, like a field of flowers. Looking up, out of the little window, it was as if she was drawn up into the sky amongst the bright stars.

Billy seemed very close in the days before the funeral; much closer than he had been when he was alive. She felt he had had a hand in his own death, and because of this perhaps he seemed even closer. She pondered on this. Had there been some kind of choice in it? It could never be undone. Never in this world undone, never. Sometimes Dorothy stopped what she was doing, cutting bread for her breakfast or washing out the tea towels, and sat down in the straight-backed chair and wept. The weeping was as if the body needed to do it, she herself was a little removed from it, but her body needed to weep as, in certain stages of illness, it needs to cough or vomit or sweat.

The words of the funeral service were drawn through her like fine wires; they pierced her to the heart. *Behold I show you a mystery . . . He cometh up, and is cut down, like a flower . . . He fleeth as it were a shadow.*

That was the last day of the ceremony. It had finished.

People said, 'Why don't you sell the house, Dorothy? Why not go and live with your sister in Stratford? It's not good for you to be alone.' But her sister in Stratford had a sour-faced husband and in any case Dorothy did not want to leave the house. Her son still lived in its shadowy places, sometimes almost brushing against her unexpectedly. The nooks and crannies of the house had not yet heard of his death. There were things in it that were still part of him, like the log box which it had been his job to keep filled.

She did not try to deceive herself that it had always been happy for either of them. Billy had been a very wild boy. His friends were the dregs of the village, he seemed to prefer that sort. Motor-bikes, drink, drugs even, she suspected. But at the bottom of it Billy wasn't really one of them, he was searching for something he could not find, that was the trouble – and the bad lots of the village seemed to have a more exciting time. She had lain awake often waiting for him to come home, and when he did she knew he would be drunk. Usually she kept quiet and pretended to be asleep while he lurched about downstairs, knocking over the chairs and at last falling asleep in the armchair. He was a wild boy. But not coarse-faced like the others. His hazel eyes were bright with amber flecks in them, and his dark hair curled over his white collar. She missed him more because of his wildness.

Dorothy sat on the edge of his bed folding his clothes away in a box. Someone might as well have them. She didn't believe in waste. Nice pullovers and everything. She pressed his shirts flat, doing up the buttons. Where had he gone, her grown-up son with his curly hair and bitten fingernails? Where was he? She looked round suddenly frantic, as once she had when he was little and she had lost him for a few moments in a crowded store. But now, where was she to look? Where? If she followed him to death's door would she find him on the other side?

Dorothy sat for a long time on the edge of the bed, the shirt still in her hands. The bedroom door was standing ajar and Dorothy strained her eyes, trying to look beyond the crack in the door into the darkened passageway. She was very tired. She had not been sleeping very well and the doctor had given her tablets but she had not taken them, only carried them round in her apron pocket. She didn't like taking things. Now she held the little bottle in her hand inside her apron pocket. Still holding the warm little bottle she put her head down on the pillow of Billy's bed and closed her eyes.

She slept at once; but her sleep was restless and full of dreams.

It had been the middle of summer when it had happened; the nights short and starry, the days long, strange and empty, stretching out in their long light hours like the open sea – empty, lonely, the light playing on it.

As autumn drew near, the garden became hung about with spiders' webs, house martins flew in and out of her little outhouse, and the apples in the orchard ripened. There was no one but her to tell her lost son about these things. Sometimes she thought she stayed in the world just to tell him. Every year, since he was a boy, he had gathered the apple crop in. This time she would have to get Harry Wilkins to do it. She couldn't see the apples rot on the ground, burrowed by wasps.

Dorothy saw her world differently these days. It looked stranger to her, more mysterious. She shared these mysteries with Billy. Every smallest thing, even the wind she breathed as she hung out the washing suddenly was charged with a different life of its own. It was as if she had never seen the familiar things about her before, they were charged with a new life – the unripe blackberry lying against the leaf, the delicate horns of the tiny snail. A veil had been ripped away between her and her well-known world. This made her shiver with excitement.

When it came to the Ladies' Circle outing, she thought she would not go this year. All the women full of sympathy for her. She could not tell them how she stayed awake at night out of excitement – as if she saw the stars for the first time; how even the dark windy nights were full of deep joy and terror as if she had been driven out to sea in a Viking boat, its dragon prow drinking the black waves. All this she shared with her dead son.

Her friends in the Ladies' Circle would talk about Billy as he had been. 'A good boy underneath, Dorothy, he always was, like his father. Never stayed in bed on Sundays like that lot he went round with.' No, thought Dorothy, Sunday was his day for sawing the logs; and we always had our lunch together with a proper tablecloth and the cracked gravy boat with a green band round it.

The Ladies' Circle Sunday outing was to the seaside this year, a seaside town she had never been to. In the end it was easier to agree to go than to explain to everyone that she did not want to go somewhere where Billy had never been. That fact made it . . . almost a new country. She would not be able to share this unknown country with Billy. And she would have to talk to Mrs. Hewett, who would sit next to her on the coach as usual. Lately she could not be bothered with words. It was as if there was nothing more to be said. But she went.

As soon as she stepped off the coach the smell of the sea was there, an unaccustomed smell. It had never been part of Billy's life and hers. With every breath of sharp sea air she felt such piercing pangs of solitary grief, as if an anaesthetic had worn off after surgery. For the first time she ran full tilt into her loss. He was not here.

It was time for morning coffee and the ladies went off to find somewhere nice to have it. Dorothy, after the strain of Mrs Hewett's chatter, and in her desolation, decided to go off on her own. She had no idea what she was going to do, here at the seaside, a long way from her apple trees and her fireplace and all the things that had held her life in place.

As she wandered through the streets without any sense of going anywhere, she noticed an elegant but homely little building painted grey and white. There was a notice on the door. This was a Friends' Meeting House. The door stood open, it looked cool inside, and Dorothy went in. Other people were taking their place in the silent seated circle of a Quaker meeting. Here she would sit and rest. There would be no need for words here. It was cool and quiet in the pleasant room, the light coming in from long narrow windows. Outside the windows the leaves of a hornbeam trembled slightly in the breeze, sending flickering lights down the white walls, like sun on the water. The silence began.

After a while the silence settled deeper on the circle of men and women, the only sound the occasional tearing cry of a seagull from the open window. Dorothy was glad of the silent company of the others who sat round in the circle. It was a relief not to have to speak or to listen. Thoughts passed through her mind like shadows made by clouds passing over the sea. There had been a time she thought, before Billy was born, when she had been in the world on her own, as it were. Just herself, strong and nimble, a young woman with brown curly hair, thin shoulders and long legs. Was that young woman this same Dorothy, Billy's widowed mother? Dorothy looked down at her thin brown wrinkled hands lying still in her lap. She closed her eyes and sank deeper into the silence which received and supported her. Simultaneously she felt both a part of the others and a being in her own right. There was an almost palpable contact with these strangers. On the other hand there was herself, still that young woman she had once been – Dorothy was surprised she was there at all. At this thought she felt she would like to get up and leave the circle, perhaps leave this new-found self behind. Left to herself she would have got up and gone, but she was constrained and held by the silent circle. Yet she wished to go. But did not. Then again she settled into the silence, deeper still, as if she had been someone who, fearing to drown, was held up in the sea by many strong hands. She floated in the sea, the water under her reaching down to limitless depths. She almost slept.

After she came out of the meeting Dorothy felt hungry – a forgotten delicious feeling. She found the others in their hotel restaurant where their tables had been booked, and she sat down with them to lunch. 'You look so much better for coming out with us today, Dorothy. It's done you good dear.'

In the afternoon they all went down to the promenade and wandered about in ones or twos on the beach, or sat on the seats on the promenade. Dorothy took her shoes off and sat down on the beach. She had brought a book with her. It was Hardy's 'Return of the Native'. She had been trying to read it slowly, a little every day, but since Billy's death she had found it hard to concentrate. She opened it now. She was not really reading. Her eyes wandered over the beach.

A girl of about seventeen was standing ankle deep in the sea. Her thin legs were so brown they had bluish shadows behind the knees. She was wearing a short cotton dress of a washed-out pink. The girl's head was bent, watching something in the water – she looked as if she was watching her own reflection. Her short hair, cut straight, fell over her face. She was wearing elaborate bright earrings which looked incongruous on this slender girlish figure. Dorothy smiled at this and at that moment the girl turned round and, catching Dorothy's smile, splashed her foot self-consciously and awkwardly in the sea, making little waves. Perhaps she would have fancied Billy, this pretty young girl. Some of the girls in the village fancied him. But he was shy, underneath, of girls. Waiting for one to catch him. Never would now.

Dorothy closed her book and began picking up shells from the beach. She put them in a crumpled paper bag to take home with her. She found shells like little cornucopia, tiny orange ones, dog whelks with their steely-blue oily colours and some shells as small and perfect as a baby's fingernail.

She got home late that evening, glad to open the garden

gate and hear its click behind her. It had rained heavily earlier that evening, the garden was looking drenched and unkempt. There were huge docks and thistle growing amongst the flowers. Tomorrow she would tidy it up.

That night she slept soundly and the sun was up when she woke. She remembered she wanted to tidy the garden.

The peas were over and needed pulling up; the dead plants lay brown and withered on the earth, here and there a green leaf or tendril left. Dorothy began pulling up the dock and dandelion and thistle growing between the marigolds and rose bushes. She worked all the morning as the sun climbed quickly in the sky. It was warm for early October. After she had weeded, Dorothy fetched a basket of dried-off bulbs from the outhouse. They were a mixed lot she had taken out of the borders earlier in the year, daffodil, crocus and snowdrop. She began burying them in the grassy slopes under one of the trees.

The sun was now at the highest point in the sky. It was getting too hot to work. She brought out one of the rush-bottomed chairs and placed it in the cool porch. There she sat and rested, where she could see the tidy garden and the wheelbarrow full of weeds. The sun glittered down through the leaves of the trees.

Then the world seemed to shift its perspective. The sun's rays seemed to flow down like molten rivulets from the sky, pouring through the leaves of the trees, to the earth which quickly soaked them up like fiery rain. The golden rivulets flowed like rich veins of searing gold, quickly alive, full of molten energy, moving through the layers of fossils, the jawbones and claws of fossilized dinosaurs, to the molten centre of the earth. Enfolded in time like a chrysalis, like a medieval swaddled baby seen in a stained glass window, were the events of the past, brilliant as icons. Billy sawing the wood, the Quaker meeting, the girl in the sea, the shells, all came together like aspects of the same thing, like reflections in a prism. This is what Billy had known was there, this is what he had been searching for. It was strange that Dorothy should have seen it in her garden, as she sat in her straight-backed chair in the cool porch.

After a while she picked up her trowel and went on burying bulbs in the damp earth.

TEACHER

~

Kay Brylewski

Across the kitchen table, sly as a fox, he watched me with hooded eyes as he pretended to read the newspaper. He was wearing the white silk muffler he kept for Sundays and his beard was washed, combed and speckled with silver. There were little blue marks like dark veins on his face. I had asked him once what they were.

'Bits of Wales in there, merch i,' he said, then, 'marked for life, I am!'

He didn't laugh a lot, my grandfather. Even when he was telling funny stories he kept a straight face while everyone else was cracking up. I think he did it on purpose to make it funnier.

Now, sitting opposite me, he was quiet; too quiet as he drank his Sunday morning glass under my mother's stony glare. She hated the drink.

We watched each other furtively as she rolled out pastry in the middle of the table, her hands white with flour and the summer smell of apples filling the kitchen. The sun streamed in through the open window, stirring the lacy curtains and sending fluttering patterns of light and shadow over her arms as she sang softly to the Morning Service on the wireless. She had a lovely voice – ruined, she said, by having to shout at me every day of the week.

I'm ready for you, I thought as I caught his eye, then looked away quick as a wink. I know your old tricks. And, sure enough, he suddenly leaned forward, sucking in half the air in the kitchen, and bellowed in my face 'Seven times eight!'

My mother dropped her rolling pin, looked up to the ceiling and sighed 'Oh, Dad!'

I didn't even jump. I'd been waiting ten minutes for him to pounce and now, without looking up from my book, sweet as honey and giving a little yawn, I murmured, 'Fifty-six actually'.

Then I wrinkled up my face and put out the tip of my tongue. He loved that.

It was his way of keeping me on my toes. The first time he'd done it, I had just bitten into a hot roast potato; lodged in my throat, it sent me rolling round the floor, my face turning dark blue. It didn't stop him, but he was a bit more careful after that, unwittingly signalling his onslaught by whistling, humming or pretending total indifference to the fact that we were on the same planet.

'Bright as a button,' he said to my mother, tamping down the tobacco in his pipe. 'She'll get a job in the Big Office, you watch!'

'Too big for her boots,' said my mother, glaring at me. She was jealous of me, I could tell. Before I came along, she was his favourite. He used to call her his Dusky Maiden, she was so dark, like a gypsy. Now she nagged him so much about the drink and tobacco, he ignored her most of the time.

To get her rag up a bit more I put on my Shirley Temple act, all bouncy curls and dimples. I didn't *have* any curls or dimples, I just acted as though I did. It must have been pretty sickening. I would have given them a couple of bars of *The Good Ship Lollipop* for good measure but I saw the warning look in her eyes.

But D'gu loved it. With my straight, black hair in a bang on my forehead, a plain little face and long, skinny legs, I looked like a Japanese doll. He loved me almost as much as I loved him.

'Anyway,' my mother watched me, her eyes narrowing, 'she's moving up to Miss Parry's class after the holidays. She'll put a stop to her tricks.'

The day suddenly darkened and I turned my back on her, holding him around the neck, breathing in the heavy, sweet smell of rum on his moustache. He had told me once how rum came from a wonderful far-away country called Jamaica, where the people were black and beautiful, wore scarlet and orange clothes and lived out under the palm trees, eating pomegranates washed down with rum-flavoured coconut milk, singing and playing drums and swimming in the warm blue ocean. He was a born storyteller.

'Tartar is she?'

He hoisted me onto the floor and stood me in front of him. 'Not afraid of her, are you?'

'She'd put the fear of God into Jack the Ripper,' said my mother, getting her own back. 'What this one needs.'

He looked at me, very stern, and I stared at the curly grey whiskers sprouting from his nostrils. Would I have whiskers sprouting from my nose when I grew up, I wondered? Mrs Jones, next door, said I looked like him, and he was the only one who knew my secrets. Once, he caught me smoking a wet, bedraggled Woodbine up the chimney. Everyone was out and I was puffing away with all the drama of a demented Bette Davis when the door opened and he stood there, his head in a swirling cloud of pipe smoke, looking like God in a bad mood. I looked at the fag-end as though a black mamba had suddenly coiled itself around my finger. Smoking was forbidden – it stunted your growth they told us, wheezing and coughing, as they dragged on their Weights and Gold Flake. He took the pipe out of his mouth, jabbing the stem into my petrified face. 'Do you,' he thundered, every hair on his face bristling, 'Do you want to grow up to be a *dwarf*?'

Seeing I was already tall for my age this didn't scare me; if he'd told me smoking grew hair out of your nostrils, I'd have stopped straight away.

Anyway, he never told on me.

Now I stood before him like Little Orphan Annie, steeped in misery.

'Listen now,' he said, 'pay attention.'

I wrenched myself back from a hairy nightmare.

'Don't be afraid of nobody,' he said and I nodded, thinking it was all very well for him, he didn't have to go to school on Monday.

And Monday came all too soon.

'I feel bad,' I told my mother, 'I can't go to school.'

'I'll bad you,' she said and ramming my hat on my head, she pushed me through the door.

'Behave yourself and you won't get into trouble.'

Then she called after me, despair in her voice, '*try* to be nice!'

Miss Parry was waiting for us in the classroom. As she walked down the line of girls, we could hear through the heavy silence the boys shouting and laughing as they played football in the playground next door. A sparrow fluttered against the window, then flew away, free as air. In front of me she slowed down for a second and stared into my face, hers unchanging. No one dared speak, but Lilly Price's eyes told me what I already knew – 'She's got it in for you!'

The sight of her was enough to strike terror into our hearts. To start with, she was what my mother called, with cold contempt, 'Cardiff Welsh', that is, someone born Welsh but ashamed of it, who spoke a horrible kind of refined English. Thin as a rake, with large, masculine red hands, the knuckles swollen with rheumatism, she dressed always, summer and winter, in grey or brown woollen skirts and white or cream blouses with stiff little collars and a dark green brooch, like a dead, staring eye, at her throat. She was quite old, older than the other teachers and if someone had told me she was a hundred I would have believed them. Her face was white and gaunt, with rock-like protruding cheekbones over which she daubed two spots of livid orange rouge. Eyes like frozen gooseberries glared from beneath a frizz of beige-coloured hair, so dry and brittle you felt one touch would send it drifting, like dust, to the floor. She had no lips, just a gash in her face enclosing a set of very small, grey teeth. She smelled of Lifebuoy soap and Vick.

Why did she ever become a teacher? We were a girls' school and she hated every one of us. But for me she reserved a special kind of hatred. Was it because of my Welshness? Did she sense my gift of happiness in just being alive? Or did she recognize in me a kind of pity for someone balanced so perilously on the edge of insanity? The pity I felt for her I couldn't put into words – I simply felt how terrible it must be to be so unhappy.

In the months that followed, we learned to know her moods. Her favourite form of bullying was verbal, savagely humiliating to her victim, encouraging the nervous snickering of the few toadies in the classroom. But in her heart she longed, she ached, to strike at us with the thick, black ruler she kept on her desk. Her control of these dark, damped-down urges was frightening to watch. And, with horror, we knew that if ever she did lose that steely grip, if just once her desperate hold on reality snapped, something terrible would engulf us all. So we worked silently, always on the edge of an abyss, putting off the day when we knew she would run, screaming silently, madness in her eyes, through the rows of cowering girls, striking left-right-left-right and slicing off our heads with her night-black alter ego.

Winter came and went and through the windows we could see the curve of the mountain glowing with the first golden gorse and purple heather. Soon summer would come, the school gates would close and we would be free to swim and climb, chase each other along the golden sands and sit in the garden as it grew dark, sand in our ears and toes and hair, munching sleepily on jam sandwiches, our bodies soaked with sunshine, dodging the swifts and watching the stars come out.

But now I stood beside her desk, tensed and trembling as she flipped over the pages of my arithmetic book.

'What's this?' Her voice, as she pointed to a blot on the corner of the page, was the hiss of a cobra – 'And this?' She jabbed with a finger at a sum with a big red cross beside it. The pressure from her avenging pen had torn a hole in the centre of the cross. Her face turned to me, pale, mad eyes fixed on my throat, where the pulse beat, wild and frantic.

God himself couldn't have made me answer. I was dumb with fright, seeing only her huge hand hovering like a vulture over that thick, jet-black ruler.

She leaned forward, gripping my arm with one hand. With the other, she ground her knuckles into my forehead, kneading harder and harder with each word.

'You – are – stupid! – stupid! – stupid!'

A girl at the back of the class began to whimper and little Ceri Jones whispered 'Mammy!' and stuffed her fingers in her mouth.

She suddenly let go of me, her hands dropping, quivering, into her lap.

'Go back to your seat.'

Her voice was hoarse and her thin chest rose and fell beneath the spotless white blouse. I somehow knew that I had reached the end; nothing was going to be the same any more. A madness came over me and I ran to the door sobbing, 'No! I won't! You're a bloody old bitch! Bloody, bloody . . .!' Choking and shocked at what I had done, I ran to my grandmother's house, gasping the words over and over again as the tears spilled down my cheeks.

D'gu's face was like a thundercloud as he stroked back my hair and looked at the dark bruises on my forehead.

My grandmother, feeding me a bowlful of custard – to her, food and comfort went hand in hand – said, 'What you going to do, David?'

'I'm going to stop her,' he replied, 'once and for all.'

I ran after him as he left the house. 'Don't kill her!' I sobbed, 'They'll put you in prison!'

'I won't kill her,' he said. 'Now go home to your mother.'

But I didn't go home. True to my nature, silent as a cat, I followed him at a distance up the lane to her house and as he knocked on the back door I crept up to the kitchen window, open at the bottom and, hidden by the net curtains, peered through into the cool, shadowed kitchen.

It was almost as though she was waiting for him. Sitting silently with her hands in front of her on the kitchen table, she looked up as she heard his knock, then rose to open the door.

His face as he entered the room was rigid with anger and hers, as she fell back from him, ashen. The daubs of orange rouge on her bony cheeks stood out, cruelly garish.

Suddenly, all the misery, humiliation and fear of the past months flooded over me.

'Go on D'gu!' I whispered, 'Punch her in the face! Knock her flying!'

But he just stood there, looking at her. Then, 'Hello Eirwen,' he said.

She clasped her hands together to stop them shaking as I watched, hardly believing what I had heard. Eirwen. Miss E. Parry was an Eirwen! It meant Snow White in English and even in my terror, I could see the funny side of it.

He spoke again and his voice was like cracking icicles.

'Leave my girl alone, Eirwen,' he said.

'Your girl!' She spat out the words at him, and then, so quietly I could hardly hear, 'She could have been mine.'

'Never,' he said, 'and you know it.'

'I know you left me, made a fool of me!' She brought her hands up to her mouth, biting on the knuckles, 'For her! For her!', and the rage and bitterness had her by the throat, choking the words as she forced them out.

Mam-gu, I thought . . . she's talking about Mam-gu.

He sighed and ran his hands over his speckled grey beard.

'It was all in your head,' he said, 'you know there was nothing between us – me liking the drink and your family the way they were – you know they wouldn't stand for it. It was a bit of a lark that went wrong. I didn't mean to hurt you Eirwen – but marriage . . . it would have been a terrible life for all of us . . .'

'Oh, D'gu,' I thought, 'you can say that again!'

'You took me up the mountain!' she screamed suddenly at him. 'You took advantage.'

And the refinement had left her voice; she sounded like the girls down the beach on holiday from the Rhondda.

I saw a strange look come over his face, a look of pity and shame.

'I know,' he said, 'and I'm sorry . . . I told you I was sorry.'

His hands dropped to his sides. 'It was all so long ago – we can't go back and change things. I couldn't marry you – you knew there was never any question . . .' He stopped and rubbed his hands over his eyes as if he was tired.

The look she gave him was deadly and her voice venomous.

'A long time ago for you – yesterday for me.'

He shook his head, then leaning forward with his hands on the table, he looked right into her eyes.

'You're a bitter woman and I'm sorry for you, but I'm telling you for the last time, Eirwen – leave my girl alone.'

He opened the back door and without another look went out, shutting it behind him, and left her standing there, her face streaked with tears and her big, rough hands beating the table over and over again.

My mother was waiting for me when I got home, with a face like thunder. Lilly Price, I thought. Couldn't wait to split on me.

'Right,' she said, 'upstairs, you, and no tea.'

Sullen and angry I locked myself in the lavatory, until my father came home and persuaded me to come out and face the music.

Miss Parry wasn't at school the next day and the relief was like not having to go to the dentist after all. The next day and the next came and went and a strange uneasiness filled the whole school. No one knew what had happened to her; the girls whispered and nudged, the Headmistress looked grim and the teachers walked home in groups, talking quietly. I said nothing.

It was on the Sunday morning that they found her, floating face up to the dazzling spring sky, in the greasy waters of the dock. She left no note; just walked out, leaving the house silent and closed behind her.

There were no relatives, except for a distant cousin in North Wales. They had never even met, but everything she owned went to him.

The whole school went to the funeral and in the cemetery, where the daffodils danced their wild tarantella to the wind and the seabirds flew high and lonely above us, we sang as they lowered her into that quiet, awful resting place. As our voices rang out, young and clear, I looked up and saw my grandfather standing by the gate, his cap in his hand, and his white silk muffler stark against his dark overcoat. He was the only one who was crying.

THE GAME

~

Nia Williams

Before a migraine she could always tell it was coming, but too late. It was the same with her games. This occurred to her on the 5.32 from Waterloo, just before she took up another minor challenge. She knew it was about to start – balanced on the edge of sense and sanity, in the instant (if there was one) before she lost her footing.

The 5.32 was a stopping train: this added to the challenge. He might get off before she could get a hold. It was old stock: dust in the air, light-fitments missing, occasional commuters rolling, open-mouthed, in the merciless sleep inflicted only on trains. It was winter. Early darkness rattled the carriage windows. The man was reading – not a newspaper, which would have been too easily absorbing, but some kind of corporate newsletter from his briefcase; something for the journey. He sat opposite her, legs slightly apart. Hers were crossed. Both stayed packed within their invisible boundaries. No danger of foot colliding with ankle.

She began the game. Not with any particular move, but with a change of mood, which she always felt to be discernible by strangers. She became aware. She continued to gaze towards him, not at him; he continued to study his newsletter (laminated paper, gold embossed logo. A company doing well, or trying to convince).

First move: she engaged her line of vision, directed it at the headline on the back page of the newsletter ('New Heights for Consumer Services'); he might have glanced up and registered her interest. She wasn't sure.

Next move: she turned her head and leaned against the grubby wing of her headrest, stared at the window, at her reflection, at the busy lights and sullen houses. There was a long interval (she wondered whether she might have underplayed her hand) before he looked up – moved his face, quite unmistakably. She turned her eyes, only her eyes, and met his; managed to look away as soon as he did. Paused. Forced herself to think of other matters for a moment. (Was there a ready-made meal in the freezer? Had she put the bins out this morning? Must make an appointment with the dentist.) Then resumed play.

The next move was a difficult one. Difficult to resist the obvious. She shifted fractionally, tucked herself back (certainly not forward) in the seat, altered the lie of her hips very, very slightly. Left it for a while.

The train stopped and he moved his hand towards his coat, which was lying on the next seat. Had she left it too late? The energy subsided in her, but he was only fumbling in the pocket; as the train started up again a ticket inspector appeared at the edge of her vision. Good: a useful break. She said 'Thank you', as the inspector returned her ticket, in a low blameless voice.

She felt fresher now, and bolder. She uncrossed her legs and then crossed them again the other way. He had let his newsletter lie on his lap, and was facing her. Another moment; then she looked at him, let a threat of acknowledgement hover; switched it off. Passed through vague disapproval to blankness. Looked back to the window.

Her stop was the next but one. The man had turned to his own window and she wondered whether to let the challenge drop. Then his reflection's eyes met hers. They held, for a little too long, and disengaged. The train stopped again and a passenger staggered between them and opened the door. Not long now, before victory or defeat.

The door slammed shut; the train hiccoughed into movement. She waited. Then looked. He was already watching her face. She turned away and saw, in the window, that he passed the tip of his tongue across his dry lips. She made an effort not to smile. Her stop next and the game would be won: she would leave the train and the challenge, hurry away to her cold house, alone and safe. She would switch on the lights and the gas fire and check her face in the mirror, trying to recreate the angles he would have seen. Shuddering with the vague thought that he could have followed her, that he could be standing there, now, patient in the writhing shadows outside her door.

And then, just for a moment, she would see an older ghost hovering around her features, and she would know that she was playing by the wrong rules.

LIVING MEMORY

~

Clare Morgan

The ring when you took it out had lights that came in and out of the stones like a fire had been lit on the far side of them. You closed your eyes tight for a second against it. Then you opened them again and it was there in his hand like you didn't know what precisely, an offering, a recompense, a gift that had its own aspect, retribution maybe, its own way of saying forever and ever, there, you poor little quick string of a thing, I told you so.

It lay in his hand and she wanted to dash the hand away behind that held it.

His cuff was a little too long and the cufflink an overly noticeable blue.

I am here, she thought, with these past things like statues.

There had been a story once, of a garden of statues that had come to life.

Well, if all *that* lot came to life, what an odd sort of occurrence it would be.

A moment only had passed and he cleared his throat to recall to himself her attention.

The small-town noises outside the window came in.

She thought to herself, God, this is how it could be, today and all days. And maybe even married to a man like that.

Who cared about politics? The only politics she knew was the look that passed between people.

What a look it *was*. What it could do. In that look was contained the whole of creation.

He closed his fingers round the ring and put it back down in the box which had a little knob on the front that you pressed, and was made of grey crocodile leather.

There was a crown on the top of the box which meant, she supposed, the jeweller was by Royal Appointment.

Flo was like that and always had been.

It had come about because her father, that was known as Great Uncle Johnny, had come down with Syph.

He'd got it out in the East where he'd been something big in the East India Company. They'd paid him off with a cheque for fifty thousand.

That was quite a sum when you thought about it, or would be nowadays.

He'd come back and married Florence's Mamma, who was a widow. Florence had remembered it. She'd had quite a thing, as a child, for Uncle Johnny. She'd never talked all that much about later, when the long time of it not showing was over, and Uncle Johnny'd taken to his bed, or been made to, and bits of him dropped off, his nose went first if she remembered rightly, and then one by one the pink tips of his fingers.

It was no surprise the way he died, with Florence outside the door with her arms crossed over the front of her and clasping her shoulders.

He'd died, according to Florence whose top lip shook a bit when she spoke of it, cursing the God that made him and the name of his fate.

All that was a long time ago and far removed, perhaps, from the room in the town with the man with the ring in his hand.

But oh it seemed to her to be so much part of the same question.

The stone in the hand with the fingers that shut out the fire was the point of it.

All roads that came and went here intersected.

If you were a scientist it would be like you had come upon the moment of supreme discovery.

The man with the overly blue links in his cuffs hemmed at her again.

The reading of a will was, in the days Uncle Johnny was a product of and, to a lesser extent Florence herself, a formal thing.

She had decided not to wear her jeans as a token of respect to this older way of being. She had on a skirt, a latter day version of what Florence would have worn but more fashionable.

Whatever it was she wore, Florence had never thought much of it. It was no doubt an aspect of her very great attachment. Love moved like God did, in a way that was mysterious.

And what *was* it?

Related no doubt to this sense of a great big gap that was absence.

It was like leaning over the edge of a cliff and being thankful, then finding yourself falling on down through the air.

There are certain other items, he said with his mouth pursed up, and some are quite valuable.

She did not care a thing for any other object but the one that was in the box that he would shortly hand her.

I am a woman of property, the voice would go on saying right inside her.

But she had been that for a long time.

She stepped out into the street and the sun came at her like a white band over the top of the Post Office.

The top had used to be higher, when she was a child, but

there had been a fire in the night, one very dark night in nineteen sixty-three.

She had seen from the hill the flames and they had looked like paper. There was about fire from a distance always the aspect of an animated toy.

She had hurried down late to catch the eight o'clock bus which still went then, and when she got home had told Flo about it.

The next day there had been the building with no top on.

Its fine turrets were all gone.

And when they had built it back up again which they decided to because it was an historic building and such things needed to be preserved, in one form or another, they had left the turrets off because of the cost.

Ever since then it had had an odd, squat appearance.

And all the new people who came to the town never knew what it had looked like before.

It was an insidious kind of corruption.

Sic transit gloria, Flo said.

It was either that night, or the night Kennedy died which was in the same November, that Flo showed her the ring and said it would be coming to her.

It was difficult to take in what that meant.

The room was lit by two lamps that cast their opposing shadows.

Outside the wind went *tic-tic* and the darkness filled up the corners of the garden.

You could almost see how the darkness would settle like a coating on the sharp part at the edge of each blade of grass.

Yours, Flo said, with the ring on fire in the dip in her hand that the lines went into.

After I am gone.

Gone had a very final sound to it that could not have meaning to one not yet accustomed to the notion of finality.

*   *   *

The years with all their myths and their accoutrements had passed.

Flo fell in love very quietly at the edge of one's consciousness and fell out of it again.

It is true that when you go back to a place the trees are taller.

The photograph of Uncle Johnny that had been put away came out again.

Flo put things in order.

Then she herself fell in love and time ceased to have meaning.

What is the nature of one spring or another when you are aware, you think, only of eternal want?

But then the notion of eternity itself dissolves in the gap between touches.

She came back to herself.

Who is this old woman with the joints of her knuckles up like a frightened spider?

It had not happened as quickly as that, or at least, only in one sense of the happening.

Many things had occurred.

There were the big things that marked your life like signposts, or were supposed to.

They seemed to her conversely very small when she thought of them.

There were the small ordinary things that filled up every day that you could never remember.

A whole life might be spent in trying to remember such things.

A life was a very short thing indeed and it was a pity to waste it.

What then were the things that had significance?

What gave your life significance was the pattern of images of things.

*　　　*　　　*

The night Kennedy died which might or might not have been the night of the fire, when she though about it afterwards it was, she came to the conclusion, a week before or a week after, precise sequence never mattered in events; the night Kennedy died Flo had said,

I am going to make my will.

How odd it was to think of a will as something to be made rather than your own self in a curious way enacted.

Everything you *did* was nothing, if there would come a point where you could no longer do it.

The ring would be hers, and the other rings, and the pictures, and the Regency dining chairs, and the carved Tudor chest with the secret drawer that somebody's famous papers had been hidden in, somebody famous himself that had escaped from a Castle in one of the times that was troubled, when men wanted more things than they had a right to, women too, it was an odd facet of being human that you always wanted, when you got down to it, more than you had.

The ring that she meant wasn't the fine hoop of sapphires with the gold scrollwork wrought so deftly on the side. Nor was it even the boat-shaped file of diamonds with the little gold-tipped claws that held the stones, so brilliant-cut and winking, in their place. It was not of course the gold band wrought like a belt with the two not quite matched amethysts, her birth stone and something she'd never been overly fond of, something about it reminded her of the drunks she'd seen in the streets, more of them now than had been, with the bottles tipped up to their lips and the same coloured liquid going down into their system to rot out the guts and the lungs.

The ring that Florence had meant and that sat in her palm like it had in his aflame in a way that flames never were in the world, or at least not this one, was the ring with the perfect opals all three in a row with the two pairs of diamonds between them, a bit flashy no doubt by some worldly standards but magical, you could imagine when you looked down into the fire in those stones Vesuvius erupting. Yes. That was what you could imagine. Vesuvius erupting, and after, the destruction of the world.

Now there begins, she thought, walking along the street away from the Post Office with the sun in a slab left behind her on the pavement, the remaking.

Kennedy had died and they had listened to the news of it coming on the wireless.

She had cried.

What a pity it was, Florence said, and the man so handsome.

Do not ask, my fellow citizens, what America can do for you. Ask, rather, what you can do for America.

Oh God, he was beautiful, and the way his hair came forward would remain with you.

Ich bin ein Berliner!

And even afterwards, when you took your O-level German, you knew it was a lie.

Ich bin was not a static thing that you could lay your hands on.

No thing was there that you could lay your hands on, not past, not present, not future, not he, not she, not speech, not silence, not even the beginning nor the end of the world.

They were knocking down the frontage of where the old Doctor's had been, that had come once a week with his bag in his hand, but had retired by the time Flo needed him, and the senior partner now was a much too young man and one you couldn't have confidence in, so Flo said, looking sideways out of the window with the grass all flat to her gaze that had been laid out sideways by the wind.

A great big thing like a ball on the end of a chain went *whock!* as it hit right into the building.

She had fallen down and cut her hand around the time that Kennedy had died and Flo had brought her there and the old Doctor had nodded and sent her off for stitches.

The scar where they'd done them up at the local hospital was white on the side of her wrist.

She remembered the Doctor nodding.

It was another Doctor entirely that had come out of Flo's room a fortnight ago with a shake of his head.

In her pocket was the box with the ring in that banged against the side of her as she walked.

Flo *was*.

Flo *was not*.

Whock! went the ball on the chain and another bit of the old wall crumbled.

Dust rose.

Machinery that was like the screech of a conveyor belt started.

When she had flown in from Paris she thought,

This is a different world.

There was a lot of water in the bottom of the hole that they'd dug that they lowered Flo down into.

So close she could have touched it, with the rain running down the side of the burnished nameplate and the ground so like a quagmire the undertaker had caught hold of her arm.

When she woke up there was a pigeon hoo-hooing outside the window like when she was a child.

If you saw the pigeon it looked fat with its feathers all out around it.

Something should happen.

There should be an incident.

She got up.

The woman whose name she had forgotten or perhaps she did not know it yet came in to clean.

It seemed to her that the incidents in your life had nothing to do with you.

The evening before she had gone to the glass cabinet with the very particular porcelain plates in and the ivory fan with its wonderful sheaf of green feathers, the tail of some unfortunate long-gone bird, and taken out the old pair of embroidered slippers, Flo had always said she didn't know who they belonged to, Uncle Johnny'd brought them back with him as a curiosity.

She had asked the question many times when she was a child.

And who did the slippers belong to?

The shape of the foot that a used shoe always has was there in the fabric.

And Florence had always answered, in precisely the same tone of voice,

I do not know.

She sat with the old red damask fabric in her hand and the light from the fire flickering.

She had said to the woman,

Will you light a fire? although it was April and had been, with the exception of the day in question, unseasonably hot.

The woman had lit the fire in a very business-like way that said,

You are a person who is used to having things done for you.

The important thing according to Uncle Johnny, Flo had said to her, is the habit of command.

The slippers had about them the very old untouched smell of another world.

Johnny had brought them back and they had lain with the fan and the porcelain behind glass.

There was a photograph of Johnny looking portly, with a stand-up collar.

Flo had fallen passionately in love at the age of eighteen.

It was impossible to say what had become of that.

She had never married.

The trap came by clip-clop, clip clop.

We would go on the train to Aunt Evelyn's at Symonds Yat and it took half an hour.

There was a man there once that stepped out from behind a bush with no clothes on and I said to him,

*What on **earth** d'you think you're doing?*

And then poor Evie's husband died that hanged himself out in the barn with a rope from the rafters.

There was a very good harvest in one of the hot summers after the war.

We hadn't the vote of course, but I'm not sure we were any the worse for it.

*And then that Labour lot got in, Ramsay MacDonald, **he** was a little tout.*

And then one day we blackened our eyelashes with a bit of burnt cork and it rained and the black ran down our faces and Mamma said it was a scandal, what young girls were coming to.

Once, there was a murder in the town. It must have been in nineteen hundred and twelve. It was in all the papers. The man was called Hodgson, or Hodgkins. He was engaged to a girl that led him on and it got too much for him. Well, one day of course she threw him over. He followed her home from her mother's that night on the path that went by the river and just when the mist was coming up

78

out of the water, like I don't know what that mist is, when it comes, he strangled her.

Those were the days when the Judge came down once a month for Assizes.

Very fine indeed it was, the Judge in all his robes, and all the other ones I forget the name of, very stately, proceeding up the town.

Assize days and Market days the pubs stayed open.

Your Great Aunt Evie's husband's brother ran a pub, but we don't talk of it.

Old Scoder-Robinson, he was a dirty old swine, with a string of bastards.

I heard tell (though you never know exactly what it is you should credit) that before he put on his robes on Assize day he'd hire a whore called Monkey Mo for a shilling.

You come back to yourself with the fire flickering.

Put down the slippers.

That old red damask has a flabby feel.

Take the ring out of the box and look at it.

Were ever such opals got up out of the surface of the world?

Yet you can make them inert just by an angle.

Blue lumps of dull stuff.

The night Kennedy died, which was the night of the fire, or a week before or a week after, the precise sequence of events is never of importance, I cried, and Flo put her arm around me.

Her touch was something I never sought or got used to.

There are more things in the world than that, she said.

The next day the papers all came out and there were pictures of it.

Flo and I sat down to dinner.

It was a dark and, if I remember rightly, a wild enough night.

Flo got out the ring and said it would be coming to me.

She put it on my next from smallest finger and it turned around.

She said I would most certainly grow into it.

It seemed to me quite strange that I would ever have fingers that were big enough.

When she had put the ring back in its pale grey crocodile box with the crown on I asked her, more for form's sake than for anything, who the slippers had belonged to.

She said (although I made it up most probably, as something that will round the world as stages do that make the progress of a fable) that those old slippers had belonged to Johnny's servant-mistress, that he had taken to himself at first for pleasure on a trip to Rangoon, and then found, which is always the danger, that she had become more to him than his life.

When the wind comes up in this old house there is a little moaning sound as it comes under the door.

When I was much younger I would say to Flo that it was ghosts rattling the handle.

It is my house now.

There is a letter from the lawyer that confirms my property and my position.

Tomorrow on the plane I will assume myself again.

Tonight what was and is are one and me entirely.

Dearest –.

There are letters to be sent but many will have no recipient.

I take the ring out of the box and notice that one of the opals has a crack in it.

Opals are, it is a well known fact, unlucky.

When he cursed his maker and his fate did Uncle Johnny have the faintest sense of how the flesh had been of her his servant-mistress in a Rangoon that was steamy?

Kennedy went all swiftly with the blood out round him, in a blur.

I put the ring onto my next to smallest finger and the flames light up how perfectly it sits upon my hand.

Outside the rain is coming down and now I hear it.

Almost you could think of knuckles tapping up against the pane.

I smooth the slippers down the way of the nap and put them in the cabinet.

The green feathers lift a little in the draught from my hand then settle.

The room adjusts itself around them like an adjunct to a space.

Breathe in the bright humidity, the scents of narrow alleys with their sudden shutting out of light.

A woman turns, goes to the door, hesitates.

I take her hand and step out with her onto the dark surface of the world.

THE WORD

~

Nia Williams

She woke up in a hotel room in Seahouses. She lay there for
a while, feeling the weight of sleep still on her, hearing the
indignant seagulls, watching the last scenes of her dream. It
was in Welsh – a long time since she'd dreamed in Welsh.
She'd been sitting with Miss Morris, her favourite primary
school teacher, preserved forever in dark-haired youth. They
had been talking, and though the words were retreating in
the daylight now, she knew from the quick consonants and
fresh vowels that they had spoken easy, home-smelling
Welsh words. She wondered how long it would be before her
alarm clock shattered these hovering pictures. She opened
her eyes just enough to see an alien expanse of flesh, right up
against her nose. It was her own flesh – her upper arm, and
she absorbed without feeling the fact that it was looser and
duller than she remembered. She began the long task of
rousing herself and became aware of an irritating question:
What's the Welsh for mystery? Couldn't think at all, and no
one there to ask. She couldn't even look it up for another
week, not until she'd worked her way down through
Northumbria and Oxfordshire, booking into dusty hotels,
breakfasting in windowless rooms, giving crisp lectures
and brisk demonstrations to pale-shaved trainee managers
who needed the basics in computer design.

She heaved herself painfully into a sitting position and
leaned over to peer at the clock. Quarter past six. Words
slid before her as she lolloped to the bathroom. *Cyfrinach*?

Secret. *Penbleth?* Quandary. In the mirror there was a thundering frown, although she wasn't angry or worried. She was turning into another person, a lined, folded person with a smoothed-down language and a little worker's cottage in Berks.

When she had left to go to college, this had been freedom: free to speak any damn language she liked, without any purse-string lips condemning her as a dupe and a traitor. Free to spring into a wide world full of other issues, broad minds, sophisticated deep-voiced men. They liked her accent in college – at least, they took the piss – 'Say tooth again, say year, say Hugh'. She enjoyed the fuss. She went out with a bloke called James who called her Taffy (affectionately, she assumed) and told her that when he had been on holiday to Wales he'd gone into a shop and all the people had switched from English to Welsh just to embarrass him. He mentioned leeks and harps and chapel all the time, as if she would find it funny. She said, 'If I were black and you talked about bananas like that, people would call you a bigot.' He rolled his eyes – bloody Welsh nationalists, bloody bolshy women. Other friends were more liberal. They reserved for her infrequent outbursts that blank, amiable look the English use for any self-contained culture that isn't welded to their own. Well-mannered acknowledgement of childish fiction. She envied them their thoughtlessness, their lack of guilt. She stayed on, moved in with a chap from Potters Bar. It was like giving a socking great V sign to all those grim skull-faces back home. She read the *Guardian*, listened to right-on opinions; free from her corsets, she careered about unencumbered by the agonies of a laced-up language and a powerful past. 'National' here meant 'everyone', meant 'us', meant the real world, light years away from a trembling huddle of streets and a fistful of angry words.

The collared and tied young men were waiting, feeling the edges of their notebooks, making desperately confident little jokes. She peeked in through the glass in the door and rehearsed her opening line, though she didn't need to. 'Now, some of you probably think computer design is only for Stephen Spielberg . . .' What was that damn word? *Antur*? Adventure. *Helynt*? Something beginning with C? She thought of popping over to see her aunt, Meinir, after Oxfordshire. She thought of going on the train, to have a rest from all the driving.

She took the local train from Shrewsbury to Caersws, feeling uncomfortable in her Next two-piece suit, concentrating too hard on her *Independent* while the mountains crowded up and peered through the windows. But still there was the release when she clattered out of the train and let her suitcase and briefcase smack onto the platform. She took a long breath: the air was different here, not cleaner but more bitter; sodden, intrusive air. Even the grass was different: tough, spiky, gripping the sheep by their feet. Meinir was waiting in the car, wearing that resistant look like slate, letting otherness wash away without impression. 'Put them in the boot,' she said, quickly, before any smirking niceties could be slipped in. 'I put a casserole in, nothing fancy, mind, you'll have to take me as you find me.'

Her house smelled of potatoes and soft water. They sat in the front kitchen, listening to new noises: the bypass had removed the hum and crash of through traffic, revealing a lower layer of ticking clocks and nagging sheep.

'What's Welsh for mystery?' she asked as Meinir fussed with the teapot.

'Oh, twt, don't start on me now, I can't think, I haven't got time for all that . . .' Meinir was flustered and embarrassed, fending off an accusation that wasn't there.

Over supper Meinir switched on S4C, perhaps hoping that the word would pop up there; they didn't mention it again, but the question was wedged between them.

They looked at some old photographs, talked briefly about the job (without mentioning computers) and at length about Meinir's neighbours; she went for a long, damp walk while Meinir made lunch the following day. When she left Meinir gave her a quick, sharp hug, told her to watch herself and hurried away before the train left. On Monday, she looked the word up in a small, shiny Collins dictionary from a bookshop in Reading. *Dirgelwch*. Of course. She wasn't satisfied. She wished they could have remembered it at Meinir's house, sitting in front of the telly in their guilty, angry silence.

A DANGEROUS DANCE

~

Shelagh Weeks

She only knew she had been drunk the night before when she couldn't find her emerald and ruby rings. The little marbled pot was empty. They were not on the chest of drawers nor on the cluttered pine bedside table. Panicking a little, while her head thumped, she sifted through the coffee-stained magazines, the books and letters. On her side of the bed, carefully placed by that morning's mail, was a fresh cup of tea. By its side were two biscuits and on top of each was a paracetamol. How had he known? Had she been that much chattier when she crawled into bed last night? Did he guess from the clothes strewn about, abandoned on chair and floor? She gulped at the tepid tea and swallowed the little bitter pills whose taste lingered. Her eyes still cast over the room, searching, searching, hardly believing that she might have carelessly lost her rings, her treasured rings. Downstairs she could hear the clattering preparations of a family breakfast. Tim, her husband's grown-up son, was calling out. Sam, the younger, was laughing with his disconcertingly deep man's voice.

She bent too quickly to pick a letter off the floor, carelessly knocked there as she had greedily drunk the tea. The ache in her head, a second later, heavily, dully, thumped too. Dazed, she put out her hand to the bed to steady herself, holding the cream envelope with the writing she knew. She felt sick from the pain. It pulsed violently, intensely, before steadying to a dull and revengeful throb. She pulled herself up and sat on the bed, recovering, counting the glasses of cheap wine she had drunk the night before – one before she left home, clinking to her husband's health, at least six with her meal, and then a debonair lone glass in the kitchen when she returned late to a silent, sleeping house. She did not giggle now, as she had the night before, sitting alone in the kitchen with her shoes slipped off, recalling the garrulous conversations with waiters, the gesticulating, halting Italian that had so delighted the male staff that a free bottle was smilingly delivered to the debris of her table. Her work colleagues had pushed aside slips of paper, ashtrays, theatre reviews, hunks of bread to accommodate the coffee, the welcome extra bottle.

She clutched the envelope. Despite the pain that pulsed from one temple and caused her to stoop slightly, tenderly massaging, she felt a tremor of excitement, anticipation, as she touched the scrawling writing. She ripped open the envelope, leaving the pain untended as she scanned the words for their secret meaning. The door opened and David, her husband, always looking a little apologetic, foolish, as he brought his gifts, came in with more tea and a late autumn rose lying across the battered tin tray.

'I've run you a bath,' he announced, pushing aside the month-old magazines with their coffee-stained glamour, to make room for his offering. He glanced down at his wife, gently touching her soft hair and making a crooning comforting noise. His eyes took in the scraps of letter, pushed quickly aside, crumpled, covered in writing.

'It looks like your colleagues beat you up last night,' he commented, handing her the yellow mug with the steaming tea that made her hands burn a little. She felt the comfort of familiar, favourite things, the soothing tone of kindness. Tipping her head up to appraise the bruised, smudgy darkness of make-up, he gazed into her young, evasive eyes and assessed his future.

'When you're drunk, the make-up stays on,' he asserted, wetting his finger and softly wiping some of the darkness away. 'The jewellery too,' he added, touching the amber beads on her white skin. She wished he would go. But when he tactfully turned to leave, she was even more irritated by his doctor's gentle intuitiveness which left her no space to be secret, bad, alone. Guiltily she watched him turn at the door. 'Oh and Tom would like to borrow your car, if that's OK, and wonders where you might have dropped the keys last night.' He smiled a little ruefully, his opprobrium veiled, waiting for the return of her strength to challenge, admonish.

'He wondered if he should look in the ignition.'

'It's flooded,' Penny offered, blushing at what she would have to say, 'or was . . .' She hesitated. 'Or I might have flattened the battery . . . I'm not really sure. It wouldn't go last night.' She paused. 'Bill gave me a lift home.' Inwardly, she cursed her own slowness in presenting what might have seemed a virtue – refusing to drunkenly drive her car – as something to stumble over, be embarrassed about. She blushed a little more and looked away. For Bill, when he had stopped the car at the edge of the drive, under the shadow of the cedar, had leant over and given her a comradely kiss on the cheek. A kiss that had lingered just a second too long.

'Ah,' sighed her husband. 'The gallant, garrulous Bill . . . Well at least he brought you safely home.'

'I feel sick,' muttered the woman miserably, watching her husband go, ignoring the slight inflexion on the word 'safely', attempting to control her body's violent response to the salty smell of bacon which drifted from the kitchen below.

Left alone, she carefully bent down, pulling up from the

floor a crumpled orange blouse. She shook it out and hopefully held it against herself. The discarded clothes looked as rag-like and crumpled as she felt. On one lapel was a just-visible stain. Clutching the silk to her, like the comforter she had permanently held as a child, she sat on the bed and read the letter. It was disappointingly brief; conversational, witty, ironically self-deprecating and containing two complimentary tickets to a touring production of *The Duchess of Malfi*. Her stomach tightened as she read the careless neutral words that had once been words of love.

When he had phoned last week, after a silence of months, catching her in the office, as he liked to, rather than at home, she had been listening to their old music tapes. Quickly she had dropped her sandwich on the desk and reached to turn off the haunting folk songs that, against her better judgement, made her wistful, reminiscent, discontented – just as she dived to the volume switch, guiltily, if David called from the surgery. But James had heard and laughed, teasing her old-fashioned taste, instinctively knowing why she played that old love song. He could not resist then, talking for nearly an hour, establishing between them the old familiar language of bantering insult, that had made them a couple yet kept them safely apart. They circled and danced around each other's new lives, offering their partners' names, lightly touching on how they lived now, hoping to wound or to court affection. But as always, if she stepped too close, he backed away, wary, yet practised in the dance of courtship that he so ceaselessly, safely played.

Penny was always a little appalled, afterwards, at what she had allowed to hang in the air – but pretended it was all on his side. Expunging her guilt, she would go home to David and with affected weariness relay how James had kept her on the phone for ages, telling of his latest acting job, the newest girlfriend, the current project. And her husband, with a raised eyebrow and scrutiny of her bright eyes, would suggest she tell him not to ring her at work, not to ring her at all. But there was the child.

They had almost stopped living together when she was still pregnant, although for years afterwards he had occasionally stayed the night, sometimes stayed weeks. Even after they had left drama school and she, tied by Cleo, had worked for the small theatre company where she did more clerical work than acting, James was likely to suddenly appear. He always pretended it was the child.

'How's my little Cleopatra?' he would demand, arms outstretched, claiming his father's role, despite the passing of a month, a year, the shaving of his head from dreadlocks to bristle, so the little girl couldn't quite be sure if this really was the man who sent all the postcards, the toys that never quite matched her age, the books with the long, loving inscriptions. She would look up briefly from the task that occupied her, studying him with her serious, almond-shaped eyes that were nearly as dark as his own. Then shyly, with seeming indifference, she would resume her play, stealing glances at the sallow-skinned man as he casually unpacked his bag. Later when he sat with her on his hard lap and offered her presents, fingering the silver bracelet around her tiny wrist or tying his red neckerchief around her bobbed black hair, she would sometimes relax a little, linger there when his own interest had waned, curious about the strange male smell, the tobacco he rolled in little white papers pulled from the orange packet. When he set her down again, talking in his soft Scottish burr, the words making no sense, the sounds strangely soothing, Cleo would quietly watch his tanned, bare arm slip around her mother's waist, claiming, usurping. Disturbed by his throaty laughter, her mother's smiling protestation, the child would return to her interrupted game of jigsaws or threading beads, sometimes looking up, chattering quietly to the threadbare lion that stayed by her side.

The letter lay in Penny's lap, touching her bare legs, touching memories. She fingered the rose-coloured tickets, vaguely listening to the adolescent Cleo, grown up so fast, somewhere down the hall, rebuffing her stepbrother who coughed and spluttered, claiming his sister's perfume was damaging the ozone, making him choke, giving him cancer. Penny could hear Cleo humming a little tune to herself and over that the sounds of the bath David had run for her emptying, cascading down the pipes. From the open window came the scent of her own duty-free bath oil, lingering in the still autumn air.

The mother felt weary irritation at her daughter's regal quitting of the bathroom. The bath had not been cleaned out. Across the mirror and shelf lay discarded beads, necklaces, earrings – a huge basket of headscarves had made an appearance on the small wicker table. David's leather-bound book, splashed with water, lay upturned on the floor. She felt too ill to do battle, was not even well enough to bend and pick up the mess. She felt a sudden fear of old age, incapacity, conscious of the tremendous effort sometimes just to exist. At the edges of her mind there played a normally suppressed awareness of the inevitability of decay. She determined, as if altruism strewn about now might guarantee some future harvest of support and love in old age, to be more helpful to the frail neighbour who existed somewhere beyond their garden hedge.

It was four soft years now that she had lived in David's house, cocooned from the previous ten of work, valium, chaos . . . and sometimes James. Often feeling as wrecked as

she did now, that other life had been full of resolutions
unfulfilled, bitter self-recrimination and perpetual hangovers.
James, seeming to instinctively know when she was between
men, vulnerable, would appear for bursts of "family" that he
could sustain for a month, maybe two. Perversely, now that
it was safely past and the conflict, the arguments, the sheer
exhaustion forgotten, she found herself recalling with
nostalgia their time together. She remembered her own mad
dashes across the country to James's place in London, Cleo
bundled in the back, quiet. When they arrived full of the
journey, the hold-ups, the motorway services, there would be
a fire burning, fresh coffee, a bottle open, the beds made – a
wonderful illusion of domestic harmony that she was always
tricked into thinking was real.

In the mirror her face was pale. The brightly coloured dress
was imprudent. She had picked it up, remembering that her
workmate, Bill, had once said it suited her. James too had
liked the African patterns, the soft clingy feel. Several months
ago, as he had collected a reluctant Cleo for a weekend away,
he had commented that its extravagance was the only
glimpse left of her rebellious past; sobriety and domesticity
seemed to have otherwise overwhelmed her. And as he had
picked up his daughter's suitcase, and drawn her to the
open-top car, he had cast a contemptuous glance over to
the far side of the drive where David pruned his roses,
quietly tending to the rain-soaked heads, carefully unwinding
the coloured ivy that threatened to choke them. Penny was
not safe against conspiracy at her husband's expense. She
had disloyally gazed across to the solid back, capable,
slightly stooping, and the words had been there to subtly
betray, to conspire once again. But as she stood, the words
ready, an arch smile already on her face, she suddenly sensed
he knew. He stood over there utterly conscious of her,

aware of her flirtation but refusing to compete. She had, for once, checked herself.

Cleo, uncomfortable with the real family group, too aware of the conspiracy, had pushed past James and offered her mother a fierce kiss goodbye, as if to break the spell. She was angry too, at her banishment to the endless partying limbo of the hugging, enthusing theatre world; tired of being feted and petted then discarded, forced to linger on the outer circles of sociability, watching, bored – and desperately shy. The suitcase and child deposited together, James turned to Penny, giving her a comradely hug goodbye, allowing his cheeks and lips to brush lightly against hers. She had felt the familiar stir of excitement, the vulnerability of wanting him. All day the awareness had lingered like the woody scent that clung to her dress. It had rekindled the memories of their illicit meetings when first she was married to David, when she suddenly felt trapped, unsure if she could sustain normal life or be a 'proper' wife. Her new husband's delight in her youth and humour, his gentle concern for her moods and enthusiasms seemed a crazy reason to have married. As the doubts bubbled up about both men, she threw herself, once more, into the safe, all-consuming madness of work which satisfyingly left her no time for James or David either.

That day, as James's car had slowly reversed, Penny, full of uncertainty, distracted by his kiss, had moved across quickly to the safety of her husband's side, her eyes blindly fixed on Cleo, who sat in the front seat straight-backed and stiff, impervious to excitement, novelty, James. As the black car smoothly rolled forward David had waved, offering out to the impassive child some secret, familiar sign, that drew from her a smile as she was driven, resistant, out through the wide gates and away.

*   *   *

David stood eating his toast, already late. Crumbs had settled on his old grey suit. He brushed them away absent-mindedly and took a draught from his stewed tea, screwing up his face at the taste. He looked up as Penny swept in. She wore a bright red dress and twisted twice around her neck were the heavy green beads that she had worn when first he'd met her – a present from James at the birth of Cleo. James had been desperately unwrapping them to offer even as the baby was born and the midwife had pushed him out the way to uncoil the cord twisted around little Cleo's neck.

'He's bestowing his favours again,' Penny announced, waving the tickets.

'Well, shall we go?' she enquired, not looking him in the eyes, dropping the pink bits of card onto the counter. Her husband, turning to face her sadly, wearily, shook his head.

'No, I shan't go,' he said, pushing some cold toast towards her and turning aside a little to murmur, inaudibly, crossly to himself. How could he begin to explain what he felt her 'absence' had cost their marriage, her desire for something that he could not provide, her need of excitement, of men's attention. Sensing his concern, his seriousness, she was suddenly jolted out of her effortful gaiety, aware of a hole they might pitch down, out of the pleasant surface of their daily lives. Something stern, unyielding in David's stance made her suddenly imagine life without this man, this family, which just kept her buoyant. She was intensely, guiltily aware of his weary despair and knew what it was about. She wanted to make things better but did not know where to begin, how to bring to light desires that barely had substance, existing only in her head, how to touch on things in the past that had too much substance. For his part, David let his hand rest on the innocent pink tickets, staring hard at them as if they might have the answer to his own confusion, irritation, pity. He wondered if he should unburden himself of the secret he harboured – that it wouldn't work, that the marriage was an old man's mistake, seized to taste youth, immerse himself in the energy of someone twenty years his junior. For several seconds they existed in the abyss – both looking away, locked in their own thoughts, intensely aware of the other. The woman stood awkwardly, stiffly, the artificial colouring on her cheeks mocking the paleness beneath. She suddenly remembered standing before her father, in just such a way, sulkily confessing some childhood transgression. Then, her penitence had been taken for granted, her absolution, the freedom to sin again. She wondered, shocked, if that was what she wanted now. She looked up guiltily, uncomfortable with this glimmer of self-knowledge. Her husband turned and looked at her with tired, worried eyes. She felt the childish tears prickle, her eyes fill.

As they moved to one another, about to talk, to face their differences or evade some more, noise erupted from the outside. Cleo was shrieking, Tim for some inexplicable reason was chasing her, roaring like a lion, and Tom was demanding the keys of the car. With a jolt, they were back on the surface, the abyss acknowledged, as yet unexamined. As she moved toward him, apologetic, she glimpsed, on the wooden draining board behind, sitting in the bottom of a sticky wine glass, winking out at her through coloured glass, the rings she had lost – her mother's ruby, the precious emerald from David. She held the man still when Cleo swept into the room, laughing, breathless, grabbing at her parents, dancing around them. In the slight breeze from the opened garden door, in the stir of Cleo's Indian shawl, the pretty pink tickets slid unnoticed from the counter and drifted slowly to the floor.

FOG

~

Susan Morgan

'Going somewhere nice this year, Helen?' The secretaries seemed to take pleasure in her discomfort.

'Just going home.'

She tried to sound cool, and concentrated on clearing her pigeon-hole. Well, the place was about to grind to a halt. Mass exodus of those with families or partners to their bucket shop destinations. She hated August at work. So she spent time with her parents. For some time she had been feeling the visits were perhaps not the best way to take time off work, but it was easy to be lazy. She was pleased to see her parents and could easily slip back into being daughter at home. She could ring round old friends.

Last year there had been the trip out to the beach with Jan, her best-friend-from-next-door when they were girls. The weather man had warned about sea fog, but Jan wanted to get out. She had the car and an outing would do them all good. (Jan was now the mother of three.) Nasty cold with Emma, the baby. It was such a stuffy wet August.

The fields streamed past, elongating, distorting into a ribbon of damp gold-brown. Late summer. The sun had gone, the air was heavy like a greenhouse. There would be fog. Creeping down to the beach, the car nosed its way through clinging cloud and stopped, just touching a drifting sandbank and scraping marram grass.

The middle child's hot sticky hand squeezed tight, her clumsy weight at the end of it slipped on the sand. The iron handle of her bucket squeaked and banged against the pebbles as she fell and cried.

They sat at last in a Nothing. The two older children seemed afraid to leave and were miserable. Jan, sifting the dry silky sand, tried to fill the silence with local gossip while she fed the baby. She was still breastfeeding, she told Helen. 'Last time, you see. Hard to give it up.'

They had been friends from the age of eight, she and Jan. They had pretended they were twins, thinking and caring about the same things, wearing anoraks and wellies, staying outside in all weathers, inhabiting a world of orphaned animals and birds. They agreed on almost everything, until the age of twelve or thirteen, when Jan's breasts had swollen and not stopped growing for months on end. She was crippled! No more walking along backyard walls, ten feet in the air, like cats at midnight. No running anywhere for anything. They ruined everything.

Jan and Helen never spoke about it, but they drifted apart. Jan had become a young woman and Helen felt abandoned. Boys lurked around Jan's front gate and waited for her after school and she looked embarrassed if Helen galloped past, still in her anorak and wellies.

Jan had early become a mother. Helen had not. She blamed her late-developing boobs. She lacked maternal instincts. She blamed her continuing education and the books she imbibed and inhabited. They were very distracting. There were boy-friends who were distracting too. She no longer thought it was a good idea to be somebody's twin, thinking and caring about the same things, two against the world. Boys were not into that kind of thing, she soon discovered. They were more interested in breasts.

'I do have stronger maternal instincts these days,' Helen admitted, as she watched Jan expertly remove Emma from one nipple and plug her onto the other, half buried beneath her jumper.

'Must be my age, hormones and all that, and my slightly increasing boobs.' She stuck her chest out for emphasis.

'They're never?' Jan eyed her bust doubtfully.

'They are! There are loads of cases of late development in the literature. I'm not the only one. There was someone seven feet tall who was of average height till the age of 22. Someone else became a giant who had been tiny till 19. We don't stay the same, you know, we're always changing. We just think we stop growing.'

'Well, maybe there'll be surprises with these three. Perhaps Emma is destined to become a monster of six feet and thirteen stone, she's got the voice of one already!'

'Perhaps we see outsize people as abnormal because we've stopped believing in fairies and giants.'

'My children were born sceptics. Never believed in anything like magic.'

'I blame food additives, given to them via maternal milk.'

There they were again, those all-important appendages. You were what you imbibed from your first suckling days. Then you did the same to your children and so it all went on.

In the fog, they laughed, remembering their childhood days, when they had lived in such a different world, an urban nature reserve of pavements, brick walls and privet hedges. Helen swore she stopped her periods for a year by power of concentration, to prolong the time of being a girl, because periods seemed to mean such a loss of freedom. And then for another year after she had left home for college.

'There's a medical term for that,' Jan said.

'No, it was my decision, and it was cheaper, not having to buy all that equipment. And it cut down the risk of mother-hood.'

'There will come a time,' said Jan, sagely, 'when the risk element ceases to be. And you might regret it.'

Helen's conscience pricked, she wandered over to the children, half disappearing in the fog, which though thinning, still kept any sight or sound of the sea at bay. She decided that she must at least paddle. She was not hot, for the fog was damp and shut out the sun, so they had all kept on jackets and jumpers, but the touch of water would be soothing. She felt she was chattering, letting her thoughts speed on, always aware with Jan that her comments were flighty, not rooted in facts, in family life. She never seemed able to ask the right questions of Jan, to query her situation. They maintained a distance.

She gallumphed up to the children and yelled,

'Race you to the sea!'

They would have none of it. Jan, within earshot, appeared and said,

'They're feeling damp and clammy. I think we'll sit in the car and have the picnic.'

Helen veered off down the slope of the beach to an invisible sea. It never quite worked, a friend with children when she had none. Such a lot to be shared that wasn't. She surprised herself by walking suddenly into wet sand and shallow, insipid waves and startled, gave a yelp which the fog immediately swallowed and exchanged for silence. The sea seemed dulled and sluggish, as if fog had clogged the works and forced it into slow motion. She bent down and undid the laces of her trainers, tying them together and swinging them in the air to release drops of salt water.

A little way along the beach she could just see a shape at the water's edge, hazy in the mist, a dark form reclining in the gentle rising and withdrawing of the waves. As she neared it she smelt it before seeing what it was: a large dead fish. She became a girl again, studying it: its pursed mouth, scaly bulk and strange fins and whiskers. She was surprised by a phosphorescent gleam on its skin as the sun broke through the clouds. The smell of the fish and the sea became overpowering.

The sound of breathing startled her: someone was coming. She turned and saw Jake, Jan's eldest, his face red and streaked with tears. He was almost too choked to speak.

She bent over to grab him to stop him getting wet in the sea's edge and walked him up the beach to drier sand where he sank down and sobbed,

'We can't find the car and now I don't know where Mum is!' His eyes welled up with bewildered tears.

Helen sat him on her lap and tried to warm him. 'Listen Jakey, when I was down at the water I saw a huge dead fish, do you want to see it? And there's the sun, look!'

She was relieved that he stopped sobbing and gazed up at the milky white disc, with clouds veiling and then revealing it, and in the distance, the sky actually clearing. As they sat there, a watery shaft of light crept towards them across the beach and Jake smiled and stood up, wiping his hair from his eyes, and his nose on his sleeve.

They walked together back to the gentle waves and smoothed, clear wet sand, decorated here and there with that day's offerings: shells, half submerged in the sand, a strand of seaweed, a paper cup, idly floating in the shallows. He, too, was fascinated by the fish.

'Do you think it's a monster from the deep?' she asked him and he smiled, though he pinched his nose because of the stench and kicked at it with his shoe before turning to her, with a sudden urgency,

'Mum!'

'We'll soon be able to see where we're going,' said Helen,

firmly, and hand in hand they plodded up, sinking in the soft sand, to the top of the nearest dune. The swipe and sting of the marram grass made her stop to put on her socks and shoes and then Jake gave a yell of triumph and tore off down the other side of the dune in huge leaps, like a spring hare. He fell once but picked himself up to race up to his mother who was standing by the car, its headlights on and door wide open, the sound of the pop music from the radio drifting towards them as if it was any sunny afternoon in August, summer holiday time.

'Bloody hell, Jake! You gave me a fright!'

'G-g-got lost, but I found Helen!'

By then she had got to them. Jan was white with anger.

'He was spooked!' she said. 'Just ran off into the bloody fog!'

'He found me though,' Helen tried to protect him. 'We found a washed up fish.'

'Don't you ever run off like that again!' Jan turned on him as if something inside snapped. 'What d'you expect me to do, leave the babies to look for you? Anything, anyone could be out there!'

She was shaking now and Helen felt some of the fury was directed at her, the single woman who could wander off to paddle and explore. As the fog bank moved off back out to sea, the sun strengthened to burn her neck and arms and she felt colour rushing back into the world and sound becoming clearer.

'Do you want me to take them all down for a splash in the sea? Show them the fish?'

Jan seemed too far away to focus on her.

'We're going home, I've had enough. Got to get tea.'

In the car on the way back the children moaned and Jake sniffled. Jan didn't want any help with the kids' tea, so Helen was dropped off at the bottom of her hill, feeling like an errant child. Jake avoided her eyes as she tapped the car window when she called out her goodbyes. She watched the little car turn the corner, a frenzied world pulled to shreds with tears and hot, close bodies.

She walked up the road, baking now in the glorious sun and passed the house where Jan had grown up, to continue to her own front garden, with its identical privet hedge and straight front path, up three steps overhung with fuchsia and hydrangeas. She knew the clock ticking in the hall would be the loudest sound in her parents' well-ordered lives. There would be the pervasive smell of boiled fish, and dust motes slowly circling in the sunny front room.

'Actually,' she said to the assembled secretaries, who had exchanged knowing looks before returning to their holiday brochures. 'I might go mad this year and get a cancellation ticket somewhere. Any ideas?'

SUBSIDENCE

~

Alex Ward

She had been looking for signs all morning. The omens were good. Two magpies in the park. A signed photograph of Doris Day by post from Hollywood, USA. A Monster Bag of sweet-jar scrapings and sugar dust with a whole humbug in it. She was careful not to walk on any of the cracks in the pavement on her way home. Nothing must go wrong.

Outside the terraced house she paused. They had been here a year now, and it was all right. But it wasn't theirs. It wasn't permanent, and there were rules. Just one more place amongst many where she had unpacked her books and held her breath, waiting. And sure enough, they always moved again. Every time they moved she lost something, a book, a toy, something. It was a real strain keeping her things together. Sometimes she felt like dumping the lot, giving them away, and never again having to care about anything.

Now her father was home from the war and things were going to be different, they said. She thought her father looked like David Niven. He was extremely fastidious too – neat moustache, buffed nails, hair clipped – shirts, suits, ties, everything pressed, immaculate. He was as polished and remote to her as the film star. An officer, a gentleman, and a stranger. But it didn't matter. Once they had a house of their own, she need hardly know he was there. It would be like before, when he was away all the time. A stranger and a gentleman.

A house of their own and a room of her own. She could

hardly bear to think about it. Out of habit, she paused to look inside the tall anemone flowers that grew within their boundary wall, and went in. Her mother was in the hall waiting for her. She looked anxious, but then she always did. There was nothing new to worry about there.

'Here,' her mother said, thrusting money into her hand. 'Go and get four portions of cod and chips.' The chippie was just over the road. She waited until a tram, rocking and rattling like some giant electric hare, went past on its way to Gabalfa. The people who worked in the chip shop all had pale moist faces like chips when the fat is not hot enough to cook them, and dark greasy hair. She loved to watch the deft way they doled out the chips and salted and vinegared them, and how they trussed up each portion in newspaper and slammed them down one by one on the high blancmange-pink and chrome counter, like a row of swaddled babies.

They ate their fish and chips straight out of the paper, much to her father's disgust. No one spoke. It was as if each of them was listening to a separate hidden wireless or watching a secret hidden film, so absorbed were they in their own thoughts. They had seen other houses before, but nothing had come of it. There was always something wrong with them – too many rooms, too few, too far from town, too near, subsidence. Since hope was painful, she had ceased to indulge in hope, but then, this morning, the two magpies, Doris Day, the mint humbug. These were signs you could not ignore. They must mean something. And fish and chips, her favourite. They didn't have them often. Things seemed to be slotting into place. She put on the clean white socks her mother handed to her and tied her Oxford lace-ups with a firm double bow.

Ever since she had discovered that the Volkswagen engine

was at the back, she expected that the car, of its own volition, might suddenly go into reverse and drive them all in the wrong direction, unseeing, backwards. It gave her an uneasy feeling. But today, she forgot this anxiety as she leaned forward eager to spot the For Sale sign and identify the house, and to look for consolidating signs and omens.

It was at the end of a long road of identical semi-detached red-brick villas at right angles to, and almost under, the road bridge that joined (or, depending upon your point of view, separated) the city and the suburbs. A low brick wall overhung by a small dusty privet hedge, a tiny square of greyish-green grass, and a concrete path to the front door with its inset stained glass window, dull now without the light behind it. The owners were waiting for them on the front step, a middle-aged couple of neutral hue and mild manner that immediately established them as modest, careful people. Inside it was the same, as if each room had been designed to reflect the protective colouring of its occupants. Nice people, nice rooms. Nice and neat and, somehow, lowering to the spirits. Their timidity was powerfully inhibiting. She felt a dampening of her residual excitement. But she did not give up.

She searched eagerly for more signs that would confirm her future in this place, but could find none. There was nothing special, nothing to say that this would be the place. And she could deduce nothing from the conventional exchanges between the vendors and her parents. The owners spoke as if they had rehearsed their spiel many times, and each knew the responses expected from the other as they made their way from room to room extracting points of interest and special merit. It was like a double act she had seen at a pantomime. They fed each other lines and laughed at each other's jokes, whereas her parents were quiet, noncommittal, and seemed to be operating as if they were two quite separate buyers rather than members of the same family. Once again, she could feel that the possibility that was almost a probability was becoming an unlikelihood, and there was nothing she could do about it. Nothing at all.

They were in the small dark hall now, all cramped together, awkward and embarrassed, like people learning to dance in a group for the first time, when she saw the long school photograph in its thin black frame on the wall above the hall table. A beam of late afternoon sunlight had penetrated the stained glass galleon – amber, rose pink, aquamarine – and illuminated it. There it was, suddenly foregrounded and familiar. Her sometime private school. And there she was, second row front, behind the seated teachers, the plump dishevelled headmistress, there she was smiling into the light. 'Look,' she said, pointing to herself. Everyone looked. Everyone spoke at once. 'Well, well what a coincidence.' 'Yes that's *our* daughter in the back row, there, see. She's at Bangor now.' 'It must be a sign,' the owners said, smiling, oozing enthusiasm. 'You were meant to live here,' they beamed at her. 'Your picture has been waiting for you to appear all along. No wonder we haven't sold before.' It must be true. The grown-ups had said it. Destiny. Fate. She did not know the words, but she knew then the certainty they embodied. The signs had been right. This was it. The little back bedroom would be hers, just as she had imagined it. Shelves for her books. A little desk where she might keep pens, paper, ink . . . Her heart seemed to soar within her. It was indisputable. Like God.

It was ages, a month or two anyway, and then, as usual, everything was packed into boxes. She hated this bit. You could never be sure you would see any of it again. But as it was to be the last time, she tried not to mind too much. It would all be over soon, and forever. The thought sustained her. And the vans came and they moved, her mother and herself into a small bedsitter, her father she knew not where, did not ask. Of course, everything stayed in the boxes, stacked against the wall. There was only enough room to unpack essential things.

Joe was getting mad with her. She could feel it, though he said nothing, his face tense, his eyes on the road ahead. They had looked at so many houses. She knew this last one was just what he wanted in every way. There was the well-insulated outhouse where he could run his graphic design business. The river where he could fish. Mutual friends within walking distance. The pub where they could all meet up. Everything as he had always imagined it. How could she explain that she had been within reach of the perfect house before, and lost it irrevocably. How could she tell him how it had felt or why she did not want to go through it all again. She could hardly make sense of her foreboding herself. 'You've got to make a decision,' he said, meaning, 'You've got to decide in favour'. But what did it matter what she decided, something would go wrong. She did not want the responsibility.

'It's very close to the river,' she said carefully. 'Have you thought about subsidence?'

LEWIS, A MAN WHO WOULD GO FAR

~

Babara Cassini

'Mark my words, that man will go far,' my father said once again, his arm outstretched and his forefinger pointing to the cornice where Lewis's destiny seemed to lie. He was the best clerk my father had ever had; conscientious, clever, well-organized, and prepared to work all hours. I'd meet him in the High Street on Saturday mornings, a big man in hairy Harris tweed and a green waistcoat which held a powerful chest and a generous heart. His head was large, and covered in light brown curls which gave him a bardic appearance at odds with his accountant's calling. 'Well, and where are you off to this morning,' he'd ask, bending down, and smiling with his full open gaze, his topaz eyes reminding me of a well-fed lion. No hesitation in my answer; this was Saturday and I knew what I was about. This day I was an intrepid explorer of the far infested regions of the jungle, a queen beloved of her tribe, a defender of small creatures caught in pitiless pits and treacherous traps. I was the dispenser of destinies and collector of tadpoles.

'Sweets and comics, and then my secret place,' I answered, squinting up, and scenting heather and the fag end of a good cigar. And then he'd make a move which over the months had conditioned me to expect a generous offering of silver. 'Here Beth, enjoy yourself,' and he'd watch me go through the gates, until finally I turned and waved before rounding the corner. The sun always shone from a blue sky, a sharp scent of salt in the air and an invasion of seagulls overhead, although we were some forty miles from the sea.

One afternoon my father asked me to deliver a brown paper parcel to Lewis, who had been absent with the 'flu. 'Go to One Sudan Villas, and don't visit friends on the way,' he warned. Lewis lived with his wife in a semi-detached house of grey stucco, ornate net curtains on the windows and a circular glass panel on the front door depicting a ship in full sail, making for the last of a lurid sunset. Through the door I could see Mrs Lewis approach, a formidable cubist outline behind the bevelled glass. She was a remarkably beautiful woman, her person now suffused with a powerful perfume which I recognized instantly as that used sparingly by my mother.

'Come in,' she said, looking down a well-sculpted nose, which appeared constantly dilated. If you looked closely, you could see tiny dark hairs springing from the inner lining, livid where the skin thinned. This in no way detracted from her beauty, in fact it added a certain magnetism, arresting the gaze, transporting the mind to picture books where animals became human and wandered perplexed through light green fields and tall dark castles. She ushered me into the front room, where a small gas fire took exception to my presence, blubbering and flaring uncertainly.

'Come in, come in, Beth,' said Lewis, rising from a battered leather armchair, divesting himself of the *Whippet Weekly* and *Turf*. 'You've come just in time to help me with the horses, the Saturday horses,' and he gave a little punching movement of his right arm to express his pleasure. At this Mrs Lewis turned on him with barely-suppressed rage.

'For God's sake, she's only a child.' Lewis countered, his voice rising slightly, but smiling still, undaunted by her fury, 'But with a child's luck,' and gave me a conspiratorial glance, which I pretended I hadn't seen.

She went over to the window and stared out, fingering

the curtains gently and rubbing her right foot against her left leg; they were the colour of apricots and one could never imagine them old. Her shoulders were graceful, yet strong, and the long back tapered into a trim waist; her instep was high, and her bright red dress tilted and trembled around her perfect knees. She seemed to be waiting for something to happen that never happened, for someone who never appeared. 'Let's have some tea then,' piped up Lewis, and he pulled the chairs out for the three of us. And indeed the table was laid quite sumptuously, with a fine silver teapot, silver jug, and matching pot-bellied sugar bowl, in which I could see my face, distorted and comical, reminding me of funfairs, grotesque exhibitions and the scream and keen of music through battered loudspeakers.

I enjoyed the novelty of shop cake. They were never bought at home, my mother reserving her most withering scorn for those incapable of making their own. I demolished several slices of snow cake, with its pristine covering of coconut, and blessed with a single cherry, but a distinct rallentando set in as I bit into an exotic Kunzle, with its seductive crushed strawberry reached only after a hard encounter with dark foreign chocolate. I left shortly afterwards, having helped Lewis with his Saturday horses, and named a few dogs.

Sometimes I met him in a neighbouring field where he bred his whippets, his small neat hand caressing their heads, his voice murmuring sweet nothings into their velvet ears. 'You can earn a fast buck on a fast dog, Beth,' he'd say. Sitting on an orange box, my legs swinging, I maintained that if you named a dog right, he would win, and I chose names from the Old Testament, strong and powerful, reminding me of the wrath of God and vast open spaces.

Mrs Lewis decided to accompany me part of the way, having first left the room to put on her coat. She reappeared in the doorway, as tall as Medusa and covered from neck to ankle in a blue fox fur. There was a reek and shriek of him, the fox of my secret place, keen-eyed, vibrating, standing there, one paw raised, the other softly poised on a bent and silent twig. Mrs Lewis brought me to earth. 'Stop gawping, for heaven's sake, and come along,' and she gave a deep sigh, as if it was all too much for her. For all her beauty and physical perfection, she seemed lonely, standing there by a dark stairway at odds with those around her, and for one brief moment, I felt I understood why.

Several weeks later, I was returning from school, and as I made my way through the garden, I heard my brother playing the first movement of the *Moonlight Sonata*. The notes came clear, softly heraldic through the heat-haze of summer, stilling the heart, heightening blooms and beckoning the birds from the trees. I approached quietly, tip-toeing through the house, and when I reached the piano I listened with delight and watched with wonder as his hands hovered and glided, his eyes closed, remaining so until the last note. And then they opened, wide and unexpected.

'He's done a bunk,' he announced, with considerable relish.

'A bunk, who's done a bunk?'

'Your friend Lewis. Gone, scarpered; gone with the cash and fiddled the books.' And furthermore, my brother announced, a sudden expert in crime and punishment, he was on the banks of the Mersey, and about to throw himself in. 'Where's the Mersey?' I enquired. It was far away, dark and dirty, nothing like the river we knew and loved.

It seemed Father had had a letter from Lewis telling him this; of his sadness, despair, anguish, for failing his fellow man. He couldn't return. I was not unduly upset; I knew Lewis well, and it did not sound like him at all, that sporting fellow with a love of life. But the following days and weeks were fraught, the atmosphere strange as men from Head Office stayed late into the night, going through books, ledgers, lifting desktops and inspecting crevices.

Mealtimes were solemn, Father's jocularities silenced, his brow beetled, and his appetite suppressed. My mother, normally soft-spoken, raised her voice, a fork upended in her hand. 'You have nothing to fear,' she said. 'You've done your duty.' Heartened by this my father cried, 'Indeed I have, I've given my best. I can sleep at night'. And he brought his fist down on the gate-legged table, bringing it almost to its knees and sending a spoon flying to the far corner of the room. He got up renewed in mind and spirit, adjusting his tie in the mirror before leaving to face the clever camouflage of Lewis's entries, and exits; sums of money which were minuscule on one page but accumulated with the speed of a whippet on several hundred.

One evening towards the end of October I had gone to bed when I heard a light tap at the window. Darkness had fallen but there was a fast full moon in a clear sky, and I recognized Lewis by the mass of his hair and his voice calling softly through the open sash window. I was delighted to see him, but my heart missed a beat. He was in danger, a wanted man. The light from the ceiling was brighter than usual as the shade had been demolished by a flying missile during a bar-room brawl between my brother and me.

As Lewis stooped before the window I could see that he was thinner. There were lines around his mouth that had not been there before. He wore a dark green cable jersey, deeply ravelled at the neck, pulled away and revealing skin smoother, whiter, softer than I expected, where a pulse beat rhythmically. A strange feeling gripped me, powerful, painful, wanting to flourish. A deep root had been struck and I was determined to save him. Hastily I wiped away a tear, for I could not bear him to see me at a disadvantage. He would be safe now; I knew that with a grave and solemn certainty.

'Got any cash, Beth? Just to tide me over a day or so?'

Had I indeed. Thanks to him I was no pauper. I dived into a cupboard and brought out a large Oxo tin which Grey the grocer had given me some months back. It was heavy with a mountainous, mutinous weight which slithered into the four corners, making me lurch and stagger.

I was saving up for a exploratory trip up the Amazon with a group of Indians, but that would have to wait.

'Take that,' I said triumphantly.

'Good God Beth, I can't take that, not all that.'

'Go on, take it, after all it's yours,' I said brightly, happily.

He gave me a mischievous smile: 'Not quite, Beth, not quite.'

He looked hungry. 'Wait there, I'll get some food.' I took my torch from the bedside, and made for the door leading to the back of the house. I was in charge now, silent, sustained, sleek in the knowledge that I would deliver him from the hunters who would hunt him down and lock him up.

I crept down the narrow sawdust-smelling stairs, warm and smooth beneath my bare feet. I felt no fear. I knew every corner of that very old house where the drovers deposited their money a century and a half ago, their flocks, bounding and bleating, burrowing their way to the far reaches of North Wales and England. At this hour my parents, their day's work done, would be seated in their armchairs far away in the front of the house; their heads bent over their respective books, and their concentration total.

I felt no guilt, an emotion that could come upon me quick and devastating, but there was none. Hadn't my father and I loved Lewis just a few months ago? And now I felt that my solicitude, my concern was not mine alone. The larder door opened, and through it came all the smells of the countryside, more dead than alive, to be sure. Pheasants, free gifts for Father, hung from hooks, silent outrage in their eyes, feathers still fine and glossy, unfurled before a non-existent audience. A rabbit hung from his last high wire, his still moist eye meeting the track of my torch, his innocence undimmed. Hams, pink and perfect, their rounded rumps stone cold on tussocks of slate and marble, and butter round and shining, sun-yellow with the sweet yet foetid aroma of things visceral. And cheeses, smiling like the moon, earthy, pungent, salty and salacious, and bottles of elderberry wine, the most potent, most fragrant in the region. I placed a generous helping of all these in the pillowcase I had brought with me. There was a deep sussurating silence in the house; outside the cat-call of a roistering reveller, and then the strains of music from the church, as Miss Herbert, music teacher and resident organist, struggled with Bach's *Toccata in D Minor*.

After that I mounted the stairs, swaying from side to side, the loot and hooch held out in front of me, the bottles chiming their last chime, before Lewis silenced them.

He was poised before the window. 'Got to go, Beth, can't stay here. Got any ideas?' I had. He could go to my secret place. He would find all he wanted there: a mattress, cups and saucers, blankets, a primus, oh, everything you could wish for. And he'd find it, at the far end of the field, a small stone shelter, protected and hidden by a hawthorn tree. He knew the farm.

'Will you be seeing Mrs Lewis?' I asked tentatively.

'Not likely,' he replied without rancour. 'She's gone back to her mother in Brighton.'

I had not been to Brighton, but in my mind's eye I saw Mrs Lewis on the very end of a long pier, in the teeth of a force ten gale, her face and body totally obscured by the flying ramparts of her blue fox fur. Quickly recovering I then asked, 'And were you . . . were you by the Mersey?'

He looked up quickly. 'Yes, yes I was up that way; I had to see a man about a dog.'

Ah, that was it. I gave him a knowing smile; we knew all about dogs. And then he was through the window, and down the iron steps. 'Shan't forget Beth, shan't forget.'

'Don't forget the fox; listen for the fox,' I whispered. Lewis looked up, his head on one side. 'Recognize the fox, anywhere, anywhere!' and a rueful little laugh came from him. And then he was gone, swallowed up into the shadows.

I slept immediately, knowing he'd be safe, that he'd find peace. My secret place, where the forest hummed, and the fields lay lambent, and the beasts gave off the scent of their blood and warmed the air, and the fox called loud and clear as the sun went down behind the strong black line of the hill. For a while I kept away from the secret place. Instinct told me to be calm, silent amid the flurry and gossip of the market town. I felt relief at the failure of the authorities to capture Lewis. Newspapers shrieked for his blood, and accounts of a lurid lifestyle informed the front pages.

I did not see or hear from Lewis until ten years later. I was at college; it was the last day of the spring term, and it was my twenty-first birthday. My friend came in with an envelope in her hand. 'Who do you know in Venezuela?' she enquired.

'Venezuela?' I murmured, and opened it, taking in the fine vellum, and a faint smell of cigars. Along the top was the name of a well-known oil company and Lewis's name headed the list of directors. There was a cheque inside, a large one, to repay me for my loan, which he had index-linked over the years. He said he had done well, very well, but that he was sometimes homesick. It ended: 'Be happy,

Beth, be very happy.' In the distance a music student was playing the second movement of the *Moonlight Sonata*. A feeling of irrepressible joy seized me; I felt I could throw myself at the sun, embrace the earth, for everlasting life was all around me. There was a sharp scent of the sea in the air, and the clamour of seagulls overhead: the green spring had passed, and all summer lay ahead.

METEORITES

~

Tessa Hadley

Muriel sat in the half-built conservatory listening for the voices in the house behind. It was dusk; the long garden burrowed, rustled, busied itself, sank into the half-light. A thrush sang his late salute from the top black knotty twigs of the apple tree. A light in the children's bedroom shone from behind pink curtains. Downstairs the adults had not thought to draw theirs.

All around where Muriel had chosen to sit there were breeze-blocks, half bags of cement, piles of planks. The base wall of the conservatory was built and the window and roof frames were all in place, carefully painted with coats of white gloss by Roger. A pile of sand was covered with a blue plastic sheet in case of rain. They had been waiting for the double-glazed panels to be ready. Only a week ago Muriel had sat at the dining-room table dutifully staring at leaflets while Susan pored in deep absorbed trepidation over which colour quarry tiles to have for the conservatory floor. 'They're going to cost three hundred pounds,' she had reminded her mother sharply. 'So you see how important it is to get them right.'

But this morning, although the double glazing was at last ready, Susan had telephoned to tell the builders not to come. The transformation of everything seemed centred on Susan and that telephone: she presided and crackled over it as though she and it were creating a reciprocal electricity. While she spoke on it she strode about the hall, her hair flying up with static, her voice raised in grim, excited exclamation;

when it rang she pounced upon it, predatory. Muriel had been peremptorily summoned on it, Susan choked and flooded. 'Mum. You have to come over here, right now. Don't ask me, just come. Something awful's happened.'

Muriel in her foolishness had thought first of the children. All the time she was hurrying things into her bag, hurrying for her bus, she had thought of little golden vulnerable heads, had actually felt them as if they were little satisfying silky hazelnuts or chestnuts hard and intact under her hands: and had imagined, trembling, the stroke upon them of mystery illnesses, accidents. How could she have been so foolish – she of all people – not to have recognized Susan's note? All the horrors have their different notes, the children were fine, only worked up and bewildered and brash, and Susan had no time for them, could hardly bear them in the room with her. She bustled them away into the sitting room in front of a video, promising them Granny would take them out in half an hour, then turned on her mother, hands flat against the door behind her, keeping the children out.

'It's Roger. I found out last night. He's been seeing someone else. For months and months: I even know her, I've talked to her this morning on the phone, I got her number. He's with her now. He says . . .'

There was the note, of course, *that* note, which Muriel should have recognized because she had tolled it often enough for herself once upon a time: he this and he that and he said, and I won't, *won't* stand for it. And in those days Susan had been the child shut out while her parents struck and chimed and rang at one another.

For those first moments while she took Susan in Muriel allowed herself relief, cool water on parched anxieties. So that was all. It was only the old thing. The little heads were still intact for the moment, the horror that had visited was only of the lesser, human, sort.

'I was going through his briefcase, I was looking for the builder's estimate. I thought he might have taken it into work to photocopy it. And I found this letter – she's been writing to him at work – I don't know what made me suspicious, I think I must have recognized her handwriting, she sent a postcard once inviting us to one of her private views, and I just wondered, why on earth . . .? So I opened it, I just couldn't believe . . . And he says he's in love with her, he's with her now, he says he's deciding whether . . . She's married too. But no children. And older than him.'

'Darling, darling, you poor darling . . .'

But Susan was only tearful for abrupt, violent intervals. Then she thrust her kitchen paper in her sleeve, filled the kettle, spattering water, and banged the cupboard doors of her new fitted kitchen zestfully, crackling with surplus energy, having to look in several cupboards before she found the coffee. 'And I had to phone to cancel the builders, the glass was going to be ready today, but Christ, what do I care? The whole stupid, stupid, bloody thing: the whole time I've been working so hard trying to make this place into something, he's been rushing off up the road – she only lives round the corner – every excuse he could make, to *console himself* with her . . . And these days who knows what kind of diseases . . . he's got to get himself Aids tested. How do *I* know who else she's been with, if she sleeps around? If you could see her – the thought of it makes me sick – she's one of those little shrimpy women, you know? Transparent and sandy. Ugh. I mean, at least you hope, don't you, at least you hope that your husband's got good *taste* . . .'

Susan and Roger hadn't slept at all the previous night. Muriel took the children off to the museum in the afternoon and Susan was supposed to lie down while they were out, but as Muriel shut the front door behind her she heard the telephone click again in the hall. Susan had made up her mind that all their friends should know what Roger had done, especially Roger's friends.

Muriel kept the children out as long as possible: lunch, then the museum, then tea. When they got home Susan was different, dressed up, she'd put make-up on and fastened back her hair with a ribbon. She was chastened, emotional, she knelt down by the children to help them off with their coats and kissed them. 'Roger's coming at eight o'clock to help put them to bed,' she said over their heads to Muriel. She'd cooked them fish fingers and chips they didn't really want, so she sat there and ate them absent-mindedly herself. 'So how was the museum?' she asked brightly in a brave voice.

'Marvellous,' said Muriel. 'We went round a geology exhibition.'

'Oh, I *know*,' said Susan. 'All they want is the same things, always: the power station with the buttons you can press, the stuffed animals. Poor old Mum, *geology*.'

'No, really, it was interesting. I learned all about the formation of the continents, and the Ice Ages, and meteorites. And in a little room they show a film against the wall of a volcano erupting. I could have sat there for hours, it was better than anything anyone could make up, you should see it, honestly. It just makes you think. These rivers of red hot lava pouring down the sides of the volcano, this sort of black crust that cracks open, and inside there's *fire*, real fire . . .'

'Sounds fascinating.' Susan stared at a fish finger pronged on her fork, then pushed it slowly to the side of her plate.

Muriel had used to be bored by that sort of thing as well. She used to take her paperback romances with her sometimes when Susan and her brother were children and she took them to exhibitions or castles or parks: as if the real world was inert and dull and wooden and you had to wrap yourself up against it in a kind of silvery shimmery dream. Now the truth seemed to her just the opposite way round: it was the romances that were dead and the real world astonishing. She almost felt cheated when she found out that fifteen thousand years ago the whole of Britain was covered in an ice-sheet. Why had she wasted so much time, not knowing? How did people still walk around the same, knowing?

She'd have liked to talk to somebody about this change, how she saw things differently: though not to Susan. Even when things were normal Susan had a way of reaching across you, mid-sentence, for a knife or a cloth, signalling with her eyebrows that she was still politely listening; or pausing you with her hand to shoot off rapid-fire instructions to the children. Feeling vaguely traitorous, Muriel found herself thinking that she could have talked to Roger.

And that was another thing that interested her: how was it that men seemed to understand it much earlier, this whole facts business? All those other – terrible – things were going on in their lives as well, they were planning their secret meetings with other women. But if you said something to them about Vikings or anthracite or the International Court of Justice in The Hague, you could see how they opened up with relief and interest. Even her own husband – who hadn't been exactly educated – had known a lot about some things, about cars for instance. Then, it had bored her stiff. Now, she found that astonishing too, the intricate juddering hotchpotch of parts under a car bonnet, the sheer improbability of it, that it all worked together and whisked you around from place to place without your having to set feet on the ground.

Susan coaxed the children in front of another video and shut the door on them. 'Mum, come and look at this,' she whispered. 'There's something I've got to show you.'

They tiptoed up to the bathroom. Susan had white flounces at the window and old-rose coloured walls and she had put in one of those deep claw-footed baths: she was very proud of it, but it reminded Muriel of her childhood, and her grandmother's bathroom, and a disturbing brown stain that used to spread like a dirty bib from under a thundering tap. Susan opened the door to the airing cupboard, slid her hand into the pile of fat, ironed, rose-coloured towels, and slid out an envelope.

'Look at this.' She was furtive, almost giggly. Out of the envelope she pulled a photograph of a naked woman sitting grinning up at the camera from a rumpled bed. 'Her.' They both stared. The woman was lolling her head back on her shoulder in a provocative gesture imitated from pin-up photographs, but actually it didn't look so much provocative as out of character, inappropriate to the sober real nakedness of the little body. She had pale, freckled skin, the white circled eyes of someone who wore glasses out of bed, small flaps of breasts with big staring nipples.

Susan and Muriel laughed.

'It's so infantile. I mean, can you believe . . . It's so unreal, I just can't believe this thing connects with *my life*, you know?'

'Yes,' said Muriel. 'Men. They just seem weak, on that side of things. It's something we don't really understand. A sensible man like Roger . . .'

And from somewhere there came into her mind an image from the volcano film she'd seen that afternoon, of a small coal-black hot puffing ball of lava, hopping and puffing down the volcano's side, exploding with little hot bursts of smoke, blasting off bits of its own black crust and spilling out its orange furnace-hot interior.

'He says he doesn't *like her*,' said Susan, 'but he's *in love* with her. He's going to decide, tonight, what he wants to do. I've told him, if he wants, really wants, to go . . .'

The white flowers in the garden glimmered paler and paler, stock and Canterbury Bells and Swan Lake roses. The moon rose. Muriel wasn't in the least uncomfortable, her only worry was that they would suddenly remember her out here and be embarrassed at themselves, their deep absorption in their private drama.

But they didn't. Eventually Susan came by herself, out of the kitchen and across the grass where she planned to make a patio. She pushed open the empty frame of the conservatory door and stepped up into the room that was not a room but just a provisional space defined by the fragile ribs above them. She knelt down and put her head in her mother's lap. 'He's gone.'

Muriel stroked her hair. There didn't seem to be anything to say. It seemed to her probable after all, that in a year's time Susan would tranquilly be watering and spraying greenfly and pinching off leaves in here, that Roger would get over his infatuation and beg to come home, that after more raw and quivering evening confabulations Susan would have him back, and that the relationship would grow across the wound until all that was left to remind them of it was a numb pucker of scar tissue under their touch sometimes. Probably that would happen. But at this moment none of these reassurances seemed quite to the point. The garden was full of whispers, and Muriel shivered at a cool wind that blew in from the open dark.

NEVER LET HIM GO

~

Pat Bonnell

A warm September Sunday afternoon. I lie, lazy in the sun. Naked in the grass I lie, all beautiful, between Herbert Williams and David Owen Jones. The both of them ignore me. I sigh, loud as the east wind. No one takes any notice.

I sit up and count daisy petals for want of something better to do. 'He loves me, he loves me not, he loves me –'

I hear my Mam shout down to me,

'Get some clothes on you, girl! Haven't you got no shame, lying there in front of the church steps all naked! You always was a brazen hussy – won't nothing ever change you?'

I smile at her, sweet as an angel. Then I turn over and wiggle my bum to the sky.

'My body is nothing to be ashamed of,' I say.

I was always proud of my body. Legs long and smooth, breasts as round and as firm as the marble orbs on the tomb of Mary-Jayne Evans. My flesh is white like the moonlight and not a blemish on it. Apart from the weals wound like a purple scarf around my neck, and those are mostly hidden by the flowing blackness of my hair. Black and shining as the mane of a funeral horse, my hair is. Only a liar would say that I'm not beautiful, lying here as naked as the day I was born.

As naked as the night on which I died.

It's pleasant enough lying here in the sunshine, though the sun never warms me and my skin stays as white as milk, cool from the pantry slab. But when the wind whistles and the frost bites they fail to chill me. You have to look on the positive side of death.

The worst thing about being dead is that people ignore you. The boys used to look at me with diamonds in their eyes, and run after me with lust springing their heels and touch me with fire in their fingertips whenever I chose to let them catch me. But now, though I dance around all day, naked among the tombstones, the lads making a short-cut home from school take no notice. And the man in blue overalls scything the grass looks right through me.

It's only the chosen few that can see me now. There are plenty that tell stories and pretend that they see me. And some that claim they have never seen me, though they see me all right, as bright as daylight, each day of their lives.

'He loves me, he loves me not, he loves me –'

Nothing else to do but count daisy petals until Evensong, not even a new tombstone to read or a funeral to watch. Forty years, just sitting around and waiting. It's dead boring, being dead.

But it can't be long now. Not much longer now before he comes to me. Soon they will cut out the turf and dig his thin grave into the black soil until the clay shows yellow. Then, at long last, I will slip all lovely beside him, into his eternal bed and embrace him for ever under the dark blanket of the earth.

'He loves me, he loves me not –' I pull the white petals from the yellow heart. The outcome is always the same, for I know that he loves me, and if it comes out that he doesn't I just add on the petal that I must have missed.

He always did love me, though he was too shy to say the words. But the look in his eyes was hot as a coke-stove, and the sweat on his brow and the glistening on his lips and his breath coming fast and short told me it all without the need of words.

He was afraid to show that he loved me, afraid of what people might say. So he walked out with a thin, plain-faced girl with lips as tight as a purse and thick wool clothes that hung stiff on her ramrod body, a 'tidy girl', suitable for a man in his position. But she was never enough for the live-cinder heat of him. Though he walked with her respectability on his arm it was me that he burned for – it was me that he looked at and lusted after – even if I was no better than I ought to be.

'He loves me, he loves me not, he loves me.'

A cat comes squirming through the graveyard railings. An orange cat with grape-green eyes. Must be a tom: all ginger cats are toms, so my Mam says.

'Pussss – Here, pussy, pussy –'

He's seen me! His fur stands up like a comb on his back. He spits like water on fire and backs away, fangs showing, tail stiff as rigor mortis in the air. A swish through the long grass and he's gone. Even the tom-cats don't fancy me no more!

One thing they ought to give me credit for – I keep the cats and dogs away. No dog mess on the paths, no cat smell in the bushes. The cleanest churchyard in the county is Saint David's Llanderi, thanks to me.

There was a time when I kept people away as well.

'CURATE FINDS NAKED GIRL STRANGLED IN THE CHURCHYARD' – the headline brought in crowds at first, but only in the daylight. In the dark they stayed away. And those that did dare to come to Evensong on winter nights turned away their eyes from the grassy alcove by the vestry wall where faint chalk-marks still traced the outline of a corpse. They huddled together and scurried off down the path, like rats with a terrier on their tails.

That was even before the rumours started. All lies, they were, those first stories. Scaremongering rubbish! A woman in white, if you please, screaming amongst the gravestones.

I only ever screamed once in my life. And that white shroud! I wouldn't be seen dead in it.

There was only one who could see me then, who could see me from the first, and he was saying nothing.

Twm Thomas, the drunk, was the second to see me. He was sleeping it off one night under the yew tree, too far gone to know fear. I stretched my body alongside him and watched him breathing through the night. I like the smell of men, even with the whisky on their breath. He opened his eyes at dawn when the dew chilled his face, and he looked straight into mine. Brown as a calf's my eyes once were, but they have changed now to the colour of sea-pearls. I smiled at Twm, fluttered my lashes at him over oyster eyes. He trembled, as though a steam-train was racing through the tunnel of his soul. He ran faster in fear than any man ever panted after me in passion.

He told it all over the village – a naked ghost disporting herself in the graveyard. Only the vicar believed him.

Then a few others saw for themselves. I was easier to see, I think, in those early days. Fear spread like fever through the swamps of small minds and for years no one dared to walk through Llanderi churchyard by themselves at night.

The tombstones are casting long shadows now, and the bells begin to ring for Evensong.

The vicar comes up the path. He sees me, though he pretends not to. Tall, he is, and straight as a rod, though he is old. His hair is as white as doves' wings. His face is gaunt but still handsome. I spread myself across the church steps where he must walk through me. He takes a long, two-step stride, over where I lie: always the gentleman, can't bring himself to put his foot on me. Then he scuttles into the church, where I can't follow.

I can follow as far as the top step. He knows that, and he stays in the porch after services, even when the sun shines. Sometimes I pose like the small bronze figure ('Art Nouveau' they called it) that lay on the mantlepiece in the big house where I used to scrub the floors. I drape myself along the stone balustrade and his eyes feast on my body, straying from the dry grey spinsters and the lard-limbed wives who hang on to his hand and breathe cough drops into his face.

The congregation is arriving now, a straggling few, all in their Sunday best. Here comes the vicar's wife, thin and pale as a church-candle. No blood in her veins, – more blood in me dead than in her alive! She passes me without a glance.

The text for the day is written in big letters on pink card in the porch – 'LOVE ONE ANOTHER'.

That's what I told him. 'No harm in it,' I said, 'it says in the Bible to love one another.'

'This isn't what it means,' he said. I held myself against him and stroked the soft darkness of his hair. The night was hot, the sky all black and starry, the air like velvet. I slipped my arms around his waist, smoothed my hands under his shirt, along the hard, hot, flesh-silk of his back.

'Don't, this isn't right, let go of me,' he said. But he didn't try to pull away.

'I'll never let you go,' I whispered. 'You know you want me.'

I pressed my lips against his mouth, slipped my tongue between his teeth. I pulled him down to me on the grass verge along the vestry wall. I pulled off my dress to show my nakedness beneath. His breath was like fire on my breasts.

His body was still heavy against me and my arms tight around his back when I said, 'Now you belong to me. I'll never let you go.'

'I wasn't the first,' he said. But the coldness of his words was nothing to the heat of his body against mine and his breathing, still stoked with desire.

'None of them were anything like you,' I whispered against his ear, 'and there can be none for you like me. It's me you need – that plain and proper girl will never warm your bed. I'll tell her where to go, I'll tell her that you need a woman with blood in her veins, a woman who can love you to death.'

He touched his fingers to my throat, his hands so fine and soft, not rough like the fairground boys'. I pulled him to me to love me again. His face was all flushed with passion.

Then the blood came rushing to my head, pounding behind my eyes like floodwater pushing against lock gates. A fire in my throat burned up my breath. A scream squeezed through from where his fingers pressed, thin and high and carrying life with it onto the night air.

A split second of dead silence.

And then an answering scream. Not human. The bobby's whistle, shrill and piercing, ripping across the night.

Footsteps crunching the gravel.

His voice, my lover's voice, calling –

'That way, he went that way! One of the tinkers, I saw him, – after him!'

The fair was in town, that time, for the summer season.

They ran, the policeman and my love, to catch the tinker that never was. I watched everything and felt no pain.

The service has started now. I like to hear the music: I sit on the steps and sing the hymns at the top of my voice, waving my hands in time with the organ. Sometimes my Mam calls to me – 'Husht girl! It's not proper bawling out them hymns like you was up in the gods at the Empire Theatre! Won't you never learn to act like decent folks!' I tell her to go back to knitting harp-cosies and rubbing Brasso into dingy haloes. I sing rude words to the tune, even louder, and she goes away. I never did take notice of my Mam, even when she was alive, and I'm damned if I'm starting now she's dead.

I was sitting here one day, singing 'Onward Christian Soldiers' fit to drown the organ, when a little child comes past holding its mother's hand. It starts to laugh.

'Why is the lady singing?' it asks.

'What lady?' its mother says.

It points at me, and I wave and smile and carry on belting out the tune.

'P'raps they won't let her in the church 'cos she's got no clothes on,' it says, in a loud voice, pulling towards me.

'Oh, my God!' The woman screams and scoops it into her arms.

By the time they reach the gate the child is screaming too, catching its daft mother's hysteria. She ought to be ashamed, the silly woman, frightening a little child like that!

The service is over. The church door opens with a creaking and a clanking and the organ voluntary comes marching out into the sunlight. The vicar stands in front of 'LOVE ONE ANOTHER', shaking people's hands. I drape myself across the top step, smiling into his eyes that try not to see me. I stroke my hands over proud breasts and flat belly and moon-white thighs. Vicar's wife steps through me with thick-heeled brown shoes: she shivers in the evening sunshine. A woman with violets growing from her hat holds on to the vicar's hand too long and fills the porch with the smell of moth-balls. His face today is pale as paper.

After everyone has gone he stands still in the porch and looks down into my eyes.

'Leave me,' he says. 'For God's sake leave me.'

He puts a hand to his chest, clutching at the white cloth of his surplice. A pulse in his neck is pumping.

'I'm sorry,' he says. 'I've told you a million times, I'm sorry.' His ear lobes look like someone has stained them with blackberry juice.

'Forty years,' he whispers, his breath not coming easy, 'and not one moment of peace. Let me go –'

'I'll never let you go. You love me, you know you love me.' I smile my pearl-eyed smile.

His face is twisted and suffused with blood. I reach out to touch his hair, so white, that used to be so dark and soft as silk. He crumples down onto his knees, unfolds on to the flagstones of the porch.

He is coming. I knew it would be soon. At last, he is coming to me. My love.

He will lie in my arms for ever now.

This time I'll never let him go.

AUNTIE CASS

~

Nia Williams

Until she was fourteen Mari hated her Auntie Cass. She wasn't exactly fond of the other three aunts, either, but they inspired fear rather than loathing. Gladys, Rhiannon and Elizabeth – three long, grey women in long, grey clothes. They would stand together in the parlour and chill the air. Cass was different: much younger, smaller and plumper – like Mari's mother. There were only four years between them. As children they had played together, whispered to each other about their prim older sisters, swapped peppermints under the hymn books on Sundays. Cass should have been cheerful and open – like Mari's mother. Her solemnity, her folded hands and quiet forbearance were an adult's betrayal. Mari hated her with the warmth reserved for close relatives. Until she was fourteen.

Until she was fourteen, Mari actually saw very little of her aunts. They still lived in the family house in Nantygraig, a damp hillside crossroads with a handful of homes and a glowering chapel. When Mari was taken there – usually at Easter and Christmas – she found it impossible to believe that her comfortable mother had emerged from this cold place. The house itself, also long and grey, looked haughtily over a sloping front garden and respectable steps, across the valley to a black forest of firs.

And there they would sit, in the pew-smelling parlour, with stuttering tea cups and clipped little sandwiches. 'Does she know her verses?' Elizabeth would say, and Mari would stare at her lap, hot and sullen, as her mother shrugged. 'It's not the way, now, Elizabeth. Not over there at any rate.'

'Well! I shall stay put here, then.'

Three sharp pairs of cheekbones, tilting and slicing the air. And Cass, who could have saved her, Cass, who served and tended and led and understood the spectral sisters, who could have suggested in her low, godly tones that they leave the child alone, let her go out and play – Cass just sat there, hands neat, face set.

Once when they came mid-week on a passing visit, Cass wasn't there. 'It's Wednesday,' said Rhiannon, cracking the words with a whip-thin voice. 'It's her shopping day.'

Mari's mother accepted this with no surprise and cut short their visit with some unacceptable excuse. As they trotted down the steps to the car, Mari twitched her mother's sleeve.

'Where does Aunti Cass go on Wednesday?'

'To the market in Trefawr, in the next valley. She goes twice a week for supplies. Always has, ever since Nan-nan died.' Mari's mother laughed her short, lashing laugh. 'I used to think it was the centre of the world, Trefawr. It's got shops, three streets and a railway station.' Mari saw a chance of future escapes.

'Can we go there next time? Instead of Nantygraig?'

'Ooooh . . .' Her mother unlocked the car door and stood gazing at the silence. 'We'll see, bach. But it won't be on a Wednesday. Not with Cass. Cassy *always* goes on her own. As far as I know she's never had anyone go with her, ever. It's her breathing space, you see.'

Mari didn't see at all. Cass had never made any bid to flee beyond those disapproving hills – unlike Mari's mother. She had chosen to stay at home. Why should she need a breathing space? Mari thought the four sisters all breathed the same righteous air. Until she was fourteen.

When Mari was fourteen, her mother died. In six months, Mari had seen her transformed from a vigorous, shining woman to a hunched creature with dreary eyes, fencing off a little more life each day. Mari would lie in bed and feel this person's disease, steel-cold, weighing on her stomach, pinning her legs to the bed. The half-closed curtains, the stifling room, her mother's closing pain – all this would tremble through Mari's mind and body. The outrage of words – 'terminal', 'incurable' – spoken quietly in the hall, smashing everything that Mari understood, killing her mother's hope. Mari longed for it all to be over, for the withered invalid to disappear. She thought of all the things she would do, of the vastness of her days, after all this was done. She would travel, learn, be loved, speak new languages, find a thousand friends and faces, go riding, go dancing, be kissed. She ached for a future.

But when her mother died, Mari's days shrivelled up. All she could hold out for herself was this same slow disconnection, this sure death, marked up ready for her, some time ahead. She moved around in a vacuum, separated from the safety of ordinary thought. Gradually, she learned the trick of ignoring the horror that moved with her. Whenever a turn of voice or a breath of skin brought her mother back, Mari found that she could draw down a great portcullis, slamming it between her and the memory. She began to cope.

Her father, however, did not. So while he struggled back into life, Mari was sent to stay with her aunts in Nantygraig.

Mari derived a solemn satisfaction from her lack of response to the sisters' grief and sympathy. Most evenings, they would gather for prayer to thank the Good Lord for giving Mari's mother rest, and for giving Mari herself the strength to carry on. They sat, one in each corner, pillaring the parlour. Lids slithered over protruding eyes: Gladys moaned her gratitude over knotted fingers. Aunti Cass, treacherous Cass, sat plump and impassive in her stiff-backed chair, pink hands layered on her knees. Mari refused to shut her eyes, refused to say 'Amen', refused to cry.

She stayed in bed on Sunday mornings, while the sisters went to chapel. By the fourth Sunday their indulgence had hardened into barely hidden disgust. Mari listened to them rustling in the hallway, collecting hymn-books and hats.

'Sleeping half the day won't do her any good,' said Elizabeth, and Gladys answered loudly:

'Neither will turning her nose up at the Minister. But that's how they go on in –' The door shut behind her.

'– in that other place,' thought Mari. 'In *my* home.' But she was too lethargic even for self-pity.

She got out of bed for the pleasure of the empty house. She creaked along the landing, past closed doors. The whole building always smelled of boiled potatoes; today there were other food smells, too, padding the house. Cass had left the Sunday lunch to simmer.

Indifferently, Mari opened a door. This was Gladys's room – forbidden territory, misted in half-light and rose water. Mari shut the door and shuffled to the next room. Since her arrival, Elizabeth and Rhiannon had 'made do' together. Mari guessed that the plan had originally been to move her in with Cass, but that a glimmer of sensitivity had changed their minds. She moved on to the door at the end of the landing. Auntie Cass's room. She moved the door open like an insult and glared at the broken privacy. How dare you. Mari noticed a petticoat draped over the back of the dressing-table chair. How dare you. New Testaments – one in Welsh, one in English – on the mantelpiece, under the framed print of Bala Lake. How dare you still be here. Mari grabbed a corner of the mustard-coloured eiderdown with a vague notion of ripping it. She was shivering with fury. 'Why? Because she goes to chapel?' she said and her voice scraped her throat. 'Because she's so pathetic that she stayed here like a puppy?' Why should Cass be alive? Mari's portcullis crashed through the question that followed. Her mother was dead. That was all.

In the far corner of Cass's bedroom, skulking beyond the window's laced light, was a chest of drawers. Mari headed towards it, trying to diffuse her anger in movement. It was short and squat, with only three drawers, made of dark wood with blackened brass handles. A flap of nylon, dull-white, was poking out of the top drawer. Mari knelt down and yanked open the third drawer. Unopened packets of thick stockings, carefully folded cotton blouses. She began to close it again but was stopped by the glimpse of a word. She peered: it was scrawled between the sensible stacks of clothing, at the very bottom of the drawer. She eased the drawer out again and leant nearer: dark blue ink on a triangle of papers: 'Lewis'. Mari took the triangle between finger and thumb and coaxed it out. It was an envelope, browning at the edges: 'Miss Carys Lewis'. No address.

Without a second thought, Mari parted the sliced edges of the envelope and drew out a letter, folded in two. It was written in the same blue-black ink – an eager, leaping hand – and dated only 'Monday'.

> *My dear,*
> *A hurried note before I leave. Returning in two weeks' time. Shall then face the music. Whatever the outcome, you must always know that I love you. Be sure of that in all events.*
> *Keep your hopes up my darling.*
> *J.*

Mari gave a resentful little laugh. This couldn't be genuine. Not for Cass. She stared again at the page, at her own shaking hands and childish, ragged little fingernails, at her long nightie, dotted with yellow flowers and pulled taut over her knees. She felt bitterly, shamefully young. Her rage began to subside, giving way to curiosity. A love letter for Cass. Auntie Cass, with her downcast looks and humble half-smiles and her 'God be with you's. Why had she stripped away this real life, this urgent devotion, and entered into the service of God and the aunts? Mari immediately blamed Cass herself, for lacking the imagination required by J's eternal love. Nevertheless, Mari was fourteen. She could sense a tragedy. She slotted the letter back in place under the blouses, knowing that, at the first opportunity, she would return to look for more.

Sunday lunch at Nantygraig was a dank affair. Potatoes and peas swelled in their dishes, moist and steaming; the dining room window clouded over, veiling the view of soggy chrysanthemum bushes. They sat munching, looking past each other's eyes. Mari felt with a shudder her affinity with the setting: the sisters, dark and stiff in their Sunday hangings and she with her long black hair and her dreary mind, Death and Grief clinging to her flesh.

'Fine sermon.'

'Very sound.'

Comments were dropped as the sisters ladled more glistening food onto their plates. Mari dodged the occasional direct shot:

'You should have been there . . .'

'Eirlys Powell's girl read her verse beautifully. She's just the same age as you.'

Mari took another blank mouthful of peas and tried to make it the focus of all her thought. Then Auntie Cass spoke.

Startled forks rattled: Cass never spoke at mealtimes. Even the business of eating seemed for Cass an uncomfortable interval between cooking and clearing up. She would spirit away her portion and then spirit away the plates as soon as the last dollop of gravy had been trapped. She spoke now and brought warmth to Mari's ears and neck. 'Maybe Mari would rather stay at home and read.'

Mari fixed her face, not daring to let it slither towards her devious antagonist. Cass must know. She must at least suspect. All three sisters had begun to rap out their protests – 'Read, on a Sunday?' 'Magazines, I suppose!' 'Read in bed, you mean?' 'She'd learn a lot more from the pulpit' – as Cassy must surely have known they would.

The heat on her cheeks was nearly closing Mari's eyes. How *could* she know? Had she been to her room since they returned? Why? To check up on her? She waited for the clucking and hissing to subside; Auntie Cass went about her duties, sliding plates from the table, replacing them with bowls of watery suet pudding and solid custard. In due course Mari was able to move her eyes and test a glance in her direction. Cass, like the others, was dealing with her food, thoroughly, rhythmically, and gave no sign of enmity. Mari had a perverse need to prod her back into the fray. She willed the blood from her face and said casually: 'I don't like magazines, anyway. I prefer reading personal things. Diaries. Or letters.' The three ghouls, taken aback by this revival of a forgotten exchange, played safe with silent glares. But Cassy – oh, Cassy was in no doubt. Slowly, slowly, she lifted her pink moon face and carefully, deliberately, she settled her bland, blue gaze on her guilty niece. Nothing more was said. But Mari was sure that war had been declared.

Wednesday. The sisters wanted Mari to go with them to Blaen y Berllan, to see one remaining, ancient relative. Mari had gathered, without quite knowing how, that her mother's family was actually rather well off. She had never known her grandfather, a heavy, bearded man who, according to the photographs, never smiled. He had owned a hardware shop, and then three hardware shops; their sale, after his death, was hardly noticed by his widow, who gradually disappeared bit by bit. First the voice, then the vision, then the memory – until she finally faded out altogether, when Mari's mother was only sixteen. A week before Mari's grandmother died, an awful cry from her bedroom had stilled the house. In the quiet that trailed behind it, Rhiannon appeared, bruised and gaping with shock. She had entered their Mam's room to wake her, she said, and, seeing her so white and calm, had taken her for dead. Rhiannon had cried out; Mam had opened her colourless eyes and lifted her hand in a faint, instinctive gesture of dismissal.

The remaining ancient relative at Blaen y Berllan was a cousin of Mari's grandmother. She lived off a thin slice of the inheritance in a dripping stone cottage folded into the moor. The sisters went to visit every year, to talk of their dear Mam, in God's care now, and to thank providence on the ancient relative's behalf for her lasting health and hope. They took a small parcel of tea, butter, eggs, tinned soup, tinned fruit, for the relative ate very little these days and was growing transparent, in the way of their departed Mam.

Mari would not go. She had to catch up on her school work. She expected to return to her father and to her studies by the beginning of the following term. She and the sisters glowered at each other with equal force and they muttered out to Parry Everett's car. He was their chauffeur on this pilgrimage, and would continue on his own annual journey to his brother at Llanidloes after depositing the three good ladies. Mari heard Parry Everett call as the sisters pegged

their slow way down the steps: 'Little one not coming then?'
She clenched herself and headed for the stairs. At the bottom
step she turned to watch Cassy in the kitchen, unpeeling
her apron and shaking out her shopping bag. Wednesday.
Market day. Mari had planned her campaign. 'Bye then,'
piped Cassy, 'back at six', and the door clattered and clapped.
Mari had reached the landing. She turned without a pause to
Cassy's bedroom door. Every letter found, every word read
would be a battle won.

She was breathing loudly through her mouth as she pulled
out the drawer and plunged her hand under the sandwiched
clothes. Immediately, her fingers were rustling across paper,
edges, flaps: at least three or four envelopes – more. She slid
them out, one by one, shedding them quickly on the floor
and on her lap. Then, without adjusting the sleeves and
straps now dangling from the drawer, Mari fished each letter
out of its case and laid her collection – seven in all – in
a garland around her knees. She leaned back a little and
sighed. Then she picked up the letter crowning the semi-
circle and read:

> *My Dear,*
> *Your note safely received. Can you make it earlier next*
> *week? Need time to talk and plan. What to say. Can't think*
> *– appalling noise from outside – my people in a stew again.*
> *Need more time. Carys – can't accept this as it stands.*
> *Can't be possible. Must be answered. Come by ten if you*
> *can. If not I shall wait.*
> > *I love you.*
> > *J.*

Mari read it once more, set it back in its place and then took
up the next letter to the right.

My dear,
Forgive me for this – taking risk – must take chance to let
you know – wherever we end up my dear – you know this –
always, wherever we are – Can't believe it can be this harsh
and simple. Please Carys contact once more if you can.
There must be something -
    How can they treat us this way the ghastly old bitches.
        John.

Mari gasped – at the word, so alien in this lavender room,
and at the thorny anger of the writing, stabbing hard at the
end of the page. Behind her gasp, the room shifted. She tilted
her head to see, without looking, Cassy still in her mac,
settling in the doorway. Mari could also see her own long
hair jerking slightly to the punch of her heart. She waited,
but there was no release: Cassy had come back. Mari turned
her head painfully and tried to escape into indignation: 'That
was a bit sly, wasn't it?' As she spoke Cassy, glancing at the
neat bracelet of letters, made a movement with her hands
only just too subdued to be theatrical. She brought them up
to her bosom in loose fists, then dropped them again. Her
eyes travelled to Mari's raw-red face, and Mari said again,
for strength, 'Bit sly'. She knew that her mother would have
snapped back – 'Yes, it must run in the family'. She thought
she could sense the phrase struggling behind Cassy's
clamped mouth. But Cass said nothing, and Mari's hatred
thickened. Imperceptibly, Cassy relaxed into a decision. She
said two soft words: 'Our secret'. Mari understood. Those
letters weren't supposed to exist. She wasn't supposed
to have found them. Quits. She waited to be left with her
shame. But Cassy stood, anchored, and watched while Mari
hauled herself to her feet, packed away the letters, tidied
the clothes and shut the drawer. Only then did Cassy turn

and descend the stairs. It was her one acknowledgement of power.

The days grew louder and darker: the mountain heaved and ducked under cold swipes of rain. Mari received a letter from her father – the first since his life had closed down. He was 'sorting things out', he said, 'straightening things up' and he missed her. She would be going home soon – for a while. And then they would talk about school. And so on. Mari folded and unfolded the page, refusing to decipher those words. 'We will talk about school.' She nudged into the corner of the sofa, into the yellow light of the standard lamp. Rain scraped the window. Mari could smell the supper cooking: broth and potatoes tonight. She folded the letter for the last time, put it back in the envelope, read her name in his writing on the front. She would be going home soon. For a while.

Supper was finished. The sisters were solving Eirlys Powell's daughter who, despite reading her verses beautifully, was hitching lifts to Trefawr on Saturday nights. Cassy stacked the pudding plates and eased them away, turning at the door to say 'Would you give me a hand, Mari?' This was the reckoning, then. Mari marched in state to the kitchen with the grim little smile of a fourteen-year-old who knows and who has suffered. Cassy had already rinsed the plates and filled the sink with scalding, foaming water. Mari's chin was up. She took the dish mop with quiet pride and began to dab at the china roses. In due course she started on the pudding bowls; Cassy armed herself with the tea towel.

'Jonathan,' she said, 'was the son of the big house near Trefaith.' Her voice was low and neutral. They could just hear the fringes of speech from the dining room. 'We met in Trefawr . . . I was with your mother that day . . . We were

142

very young . . . He was a gentle boy.' Each sentence was placed to one side with each gleaming plate. The tea towel snapped and flicked without a pause. Mari mopped at the bowls and waited. 'Well, they didn't like it. Mam was ill, then, of course, dying. They said I was frivolous. Elizabeth didn't like it at all. After Mam died they put a stop to it.'

Mari asked, 'Why did you listen to them?' and managed not to sneer. Cassy dealt the plates into the corner cupboard. She began to wipe the bowls.

'We needed each other. As family. Mam had passed on. Your mother was still a – well, still young. We had to stick together, didn't we. And Jonathan was going away.'

Mari emptied the sink. The water's grunts and hiccoughs almost drowned Cassy's words. Mari moved closer to her and dried her hands on the tea towel.

'He wanted me to go with him, you see. He wanted us to get married. They wouldn't have it. Well – we were very young.'

She looked at her niece for the first time since starting her tale. Her expression was padlocked and smooth. 'I had to stay.'

When Mari went home her father was courteous but unsteady. She was to go to a girls' boarding school: the best solution all round. She watched her father stuttering from room to room, feeling his way with undecided hands, and accepted the solution. Within three weeks she had been loaded into the car with her term's cargo and shipped off to a place of buzzing corridors and shiny floors. The cloak of tragedy that hung around her proved a useful substitute for friendship. Other pupils stood apart with respect. On the whole she was let alone, which suited Mari very well. She learned to negotiate the fretwork of codes and duties that shut out the world; she learned to pass out confidences and affections in appropriate rations. Mari made it to the sixth form with barely a scratch. Every night for four years she hugged to herself the secret of Aunt Cassy's silent life. Every night, unable to sketch her mother's faded features, she drew the calm line of Cassy's face.

In the holidays Mari always returned to Nantygraig. She became tolerant of the sisters, modelling her patience on her aunt's. She could have despised them for imprisoning Cass in drudgery and prayer. But there was a sharper appeal in the martyr's courage. Mari found at last that she could not even dream of her mother. The portcullis had come down for good. Instead, she dreamed of her aunt, of her purity and sacrifice. Cassy had transcended the dreariness of daily life. She offered the certainty of a saint.

A couple sat in the National Milk Bar, huddled in misery. He stirred and stirred his tea. She let her vision rest against the grey window. Nobody outside. One other customer inside: a curved old man, growling gently in the far corner. Mari touched her companion's hand and the stirring stopped. He kept hold of the spoon, spoke to it: 'There's no reason on earth why you shouldn't come.'

Mari rested her cheek on her hand and watched his fair head. The spoon began another circuit.

'I've got family,' she said. 'They're getting on.'

'Well, people come back, on holiday, it's not unheard of.'

His voice was muffled and petulant. Mari said quickly: 'We're not talking about Cardiff, are we. Or London, even. Anyway –' She turned to the window again.

'Anyway . . .?' He lifted his face, challenging her self-control. Mari shook her head, then changed her mind.

'Anyway. It doesn't seem to make a great deal of difference. You've taken the job.'

He rapped the teaspoon into the saucer. 'What choice did I have?'

The growling old man shifted round in his seat and searched for the raised voice. Mari said, quietly, 'I mean, *you* don't have to worry. Your decision's been made. Whatever I do.'

He crouched over his tea again. She wondered whether he might cry. 'It's not *Mars*, Mari. Lots of people go to New Zealand and still come back for visits. *Loads* of people. You can't be shackled to your bloody aunts for ever.'

Mari pushed back her seat, balanced her fingers on the table edge. 'I don't know,' she said. 'Give me some time.'

'You mustn't stay.' Then Cassy's face and voice hardened. 'You – must – go.' She measured and delivered the words as if aiming a careful blow. Mari watched her, waiting for a meaning. Eventually she offered her own. 'Auntie Cass, it won't be the same for me. Nobody's tried to stop me and I'm not bitter about anything. It's my own choice.' Her aunt moved her head irritably and began to prepare for the Wednesday outing. Folded carrier bag; trolley; raincoat. She said: 'And you'd better come with me today.' As though that were another task on her list. 'Come to the market?' Blasphemy. 'You always go on your own.' Every week, every year, for thirty-nine years. Her private afternoons – a few hours of meditation and regret. Auntie Cass said nothing and Mari, knowing defeat, lifted her meek jacket from the back of the chair.

They took the 103 bus to the station. Mari said, 'What happens if the bus doesn't run?'

'It always runs.' Then she relented. 'Once I had a lift from Terry Round-Back.' Terry Round-Back drove a butcher's van along the valley and had a perfectly upright posture. He was known for his extended visits to willing female customers, who gave surreptitious access by the back door.

They had a seven minute wait for the branch line to Trefawr. Auntie Cass sat on the platform bench, clutching the bar of her trolley as though there were strangers there. Six other people boarded the train: every one greeted Cass but shied obediently from conversation.

There was a long, uphill walk from the station to the market. The air was smoky and hung with a feeble drizzle. Cass and Mari moved among the stalls and the shouts and the loud shopping women and the pipe-smoking men. Cass made no further reference to Mari's decision. She squeezed the fruit, eyed the fish, filled the carrier with fresh food and the trolley with tins and preserves. Mari limped behind her with the carrier bag and wondered whether this impractically large haul was just for effect. Finally, Cassy stopped at the edge of the market and adjusted her see-through bonnet. She said over her shoulder, 'Right. Come on,' and trundled the wrong way up the High Street.

'Where are we going?' gasped Mari, lurching with the carrier, convinced that she was being punished. Cass plodded on in silence. The trolley rumbled at her heels. They turned the corner and reached the quieter end of town. Then she veered left, up a narrow, steeper street, and laboured on. The houses petered out. Then there were no buildings at all. They turned again, onto a gravel track, wet and thick with overhanging trees. Mari transferred the carrier to her left hand and the rhythmic smack of its load to her left thigh. The track continued up the mountain, swerved impulsively to the left just before the summit. Mari stopped, let the carrier bag attach itself to the ground, arched her cramped back. A glint of light at her side made her turn round to see the valley they had left behind. The town was a grey-and-red clutter hammocked in green. 'Come along, then,' called Cassy, now out of sight. Mari turned with the track and the shrubbery closed in. They fussed along it, dripping and silent, until the hedges drew back to reveal a gate and a small, shabby cottage.

Cassy stood at the cottage door and fished among the contents of her handbag. She pulled out a keyring with two keys and unlocked the door. Mari followed, shivering, straight into the small front room. 'Here we are,' said Cass. She parked the trolley in a corner and, before taking off her raincoat and bonnet, squatted on the hearth to light the fire. A box of Swan matches and a poker were set ready on the quarry tiles. There was a square table at the netted window, covered with a white embroidered cloth. Two chairs, one on each side. A dresser by the door into the kitchen, with a few items of faded crockery. A clock tutting ponderously on the mantelpiece. Nothing else. The fire sizzled. Cassy got to her feet in stages and shook off her rainwear. 'We came here,' she said, 'to say goodbye.' Mari sat heavily by the table and ran her hand over her wet hair. 'It's an estate cottage,' said Cass, raising her voice as she took her coat to the kitchen. 'But it had been empty for years and years, even then.'

Mari heard the rush and clink of the kettle being filled and put on the hob. Then she heard a firm suck of gravel. She squinted round the net curtain. A car had stopped a short distance beyond the cottage. A bulky male figure climbed out and clacked the door shut. 'Auntie Cass,' she called, and jumped to find Cass at her elbow, laying the table for tea.

The man walked slowly to the door, bothered it with a key and came in. He smiled at Cass; widened his eyes at Mari. Cass said, 'She had to come with me,' and steadied him with a look that seemed also to be an explanation. He was a large, balding man with neat features and a broad face, reddened with age and comfort. He wore a soft tweed jacket and corduroy trousers. He nodded bashfully to Mari and crossed to the other seat – obviously not his usual place.

'Tea's coming, now-just,' said Cass and returned to the kitchen. 'Well then!' said the man, loudly, to Mari. 'It's a soggy old day!' 'Yes,' said Mari, and found that she was winding one corner of the tablecloth tightly round her finger. They waited, let the clock slice up the silence. Cass came back carrying a tray with teapot, milk jug, strainer, plate of bread and butter. She spoke as she set them out. 'Jonathan, there's a stool in the back. That'll do for a third.' Jonathan struggled past her and into the kitchen. 'We thought we would come here, just once, to say goodbye,' said Cass, in her efficient way. Jonathan filled the room again, carrying a weightless three-legged stool. 'I could hardly bear it, you know,' he added cheerfully. Cass said, 'I wouldn't bear it at all.'

Mari saw her aunt's conclusive face and understood. Cassy had decided. Cassy had said the word and he, of course, had obeyed. So every week, for thirty-nine years, they had met here, in their own home.

'Doesn't *anyone* know?' Cass and Jonathan exchanged a mild, questioning look and Cassy shrugged. 'At any rate, no one who's anyone to us.' Mari stood to offer her aunt the chair but Jonathan was quicker. He balanced himself improbably on the stool. Cassy sat nearest the fire and poured the tea.

'You must go with your . . . friend.' She handed Mari a cup. 'Don't think for *one minute* that there's virtue in loneliness. I've been content. Twice a week, every week, I've had my companion.' 'And twice a week's as good as a feast, eh!' bawled Jonathan.'If I had stayed there alone,' said Cassy, 'I would have died.' Mari watched her pour Jonathan's tea.

The old hatred touched her, tightened her jaw. She said, 'Don't worry. I'm not staying,' but she knew that she would not go with him. Sitting in this small corner of Cassy's life, Mari recognized a fragment of the horror that had dogged her fourteen-year-old days.

In due course, Jonathan cleared his throat, and Mari took this as a signal for speech. 'What will you do,' she said, 'when . . . you know, it's a long old climb up that hill.' Cass took the point with a dip of the head. 'Oh, there's not long to go now. Won't be long and we can move in for good if we want to.' Uneasy, Jonathan wheezed and slid Cass a schoolboy look. Cass went on, 'We don't mind about people here. They don't bother us.' Mari realized with a jolt that, somewhere along the line, they had been married. 'As for the girls' – Cass was pouring more tea – 'Well, well. They won't last long now. Elizabeth's halfway to the other side already; God bless her.' Auntie Cass nodded her slow, pious nod as she took the last slice of bread.

SKIN EATERS

~

Elizabeth Baines

From across the table, she watched how he ate. He was eating mackerel. He ate delicately for a big man, balancing the instruments in enormous hands, carefully prising. His mouth, which when relaxed was soft and wide and revealed long teeth, in eating became narrow and fastidious. He sucked his cheeks, and you could see his savouring.

He looked up. 'How is yours?'

'Oh, yes!' she said, startled, remembering her own food. 'It's very good.'

He looked up intently for a moment to satisfy himself that that was so, and then turned his attention back to the fish. He slipped his knife under the glistening muscle, and lifted it away from the skin. When he'd finished, there on the plate lay the limp, bruised skin.

He wiped his mouth.

She said, 'I see you leave the skin.'

He looked surprised, and then laughed, displaying his teeth. 'Don't you?'

'No, I don't. It's the best bit! The tastiest, a taste to be cultivated, and also the part most full of vitamins. I always eat the skin.'

'You gobble everything up?' And they both laughed then, and reached across the table, and took hands.

Her hand was lost in his, embedded. He said to her softly: 'Will you come to my house?'

This was the curled-up end of summer. They walked the streets, arm in arm, where cars slammed past and flapped sheets of rough air, and then into a suburb of trees with dry tongues.

He showed her in through the door, and clicked it shut behind them. The city was shut out, and in the hall there was silence. The stair curved up maybe four storeys.

She went to look round. She clonked up and down and found boxes and dust, and files and papers in odd places like lavatories, and faded unused bedrooms. She came back to where he was brewing the coffee and said, 'This enormous house, and you live all alone?'

He smiled with his mouth closed and brought her her coffee. He had taken off his jacket and rolled up his shirt-sleeves. He was stout with middle age, something she was not used to in a lover. He set the coffee aside and took her fast in his arms, and her smallness dissolved in his pressing bulk.

She asked again, blowing on her coffee, 'So many beds, and you live alone?'

And this time he told her: 'There was once a woman, and also some children, but now they are gone.'

He was silent then, and she sensed he felt she should not go on. She paused in her drinking, and wondered at that. He was sparing her feelings. He had not yet grasped that she was fearless and open, accepted anything willingly, as she willingly yielded to the strangeness of his vast sheeny body, and the rigid power of his circumcision, with no soft, quick skin.

The next morning he said: 'Why don't you stay?'

She was mellow from the night before, and today was the weekend: she would stay. She would stay in this house, shut off from the city.

He said, 'What shall I cook?'

She said, 'Fish and chips will do.'

He said, 'No, I will cook you special meals; delicate meals, with fine-blended flavours. I only want the best for you.'

Her heart lurched a little then, and she thought that she loved him – for sparing her feelings, and for wanting the best for her.

He went off to the shops with a basket on his arm and his trouser-legs flapping, to buy garlic and cream and tomatoes shaped like pumpkins and a sprig of fresh marjoram. She watched from the bay-fronted bedroom as he went out of sight down beyond the trees. She stood a while after he had disappeared, watching odd leaves unpick themselves from the trees and drift away across the view. She missed him when he had gone, and felt lonely with the heights and depths of the house at her back.

At last she turned in. She wandered round once more. And this time she wondered that in none of the rooms was there anything to show that a wife and children had once been there – not a toy, nor a poster, no magazines or photographs. The rooms were bleak, devoid of identity. And strangely, once this had struck her, she felt the need to creep around carefully and not make any sound. She ran a bath, and the sound of the water rushing onto the enamel made her nervous, made her look round and strain her ears, and once she was immersed she lay still, hardly breathing, so that the skin of the water lay intact.

Finally noises below told her he was back, and by the time she was dressed herbal aromas were drifting up the stairs. She went down.

He looked up with a smile. 'It's so homely to hear you clattering around upstairs.'

And it crossed her mind that she had missed a room somewhere, and that he had forgotten to tell her that he shared the house with someone else.

The meal was delicious. Special ingredients, carefully prepared. Yes, fish and chps would have done her nicely, but she knew how to appreciate fine food when she got it. He served it with a flourish, huge palms open, offering.

She took her first mouthful.

'Delicious,' she said. She saw his mouth close in firm satisfaction.

She had passed a test.

And she'd been expected to pass it: he had expected her to approve.

Well, she did. She found it all exquisite. Yet in the night she woke to nausea. At length it passed off, and she lay in relief, hearing the scraping of leaves outside.

He was roused by her wakefulness. She said that the wind on the leaves had disturbed her, and embracing her he sleepily whispered: 'You are such a little timid one, everything you come across makes you afraid.'

As though he were thinking of somebody else.

Not of her at all.

Yet he followed that line when they rose in the early hours to make a pot of tea. He said again, fondly: 'You are a scared little thing.'

She cried in amazement: 'I am scared of nothing!'

He nodded knowingly, pouring out the tea, letting it fall from a height and make a tearing sound.

He said, 'You should take things as they come!'

'But so I do! I am open to everything!'

He nodded again. 'That's just where you're vulnerable. You're too keen to enjoy. You're scared stiff not to.'

And it seemed to her suddenly, yes, he was right.

She shivered. Near-naked in autumn in an unheated

kitchen, she was getting very cold. He softened and lost his mocking manner, and got up and went across to the door where there were hooks and garments hanging, and he took one, and brought it back and laid it gently over her shoulders, and his tenderness told her that it was for this that he loved her: her vulnerability, which she had not recognized until he had prised it out for her.

And she continued to shiver, because all he had brought her was an old grey shirt, cotton, of no substance.

The next day he cherished her, made luxurious love to her, and brought her food in bed. Wholemeal bread and a variety of cheeses. He said: 'I got this one specially, I know you will like it, it's Cheddar smoked with paprika.' He cut off a slice.

She bit into the sliver. Tartness and richness broke together on her palate.

'I'm sorry,' she said, 'I can't eat any more.'

'Come, come,' he said, teasing, 'you must gobble up everything.' And loving her distress, loving her for needing him, he gathered her up into his great bear-arms.

Her head was trapped above the plate and the kippered smell of the cheese was caught in her throat. She turned to be free, and her eye lit on something lying on the floor. A garment like a husk, shrivelled and colourless: the shirt he had slipped on her shoulders in the night. And now in the daylight she saw it was a woman's shirt, the shirt that a woman had once left behind.

He sensed her rigidity, and looked to see what had caught her attention. He closed his mouth and fastidiously hid the fact that he was smiling.

And she knew with a quick little hardening of her heart that this was one skin she was going to leave behind.

THE TON-Y-MYNYDD TOYBOY

~

Jenny Sullivan

I tell you, seeing Willie Probert again tonight really shook me up. It looks like he achieved his ambition – but then again . . .

Better start at the beginning, I suppose. Job prospects wasn't what you might call good in Ton-y-Mynydd in the late fifties. There was the local shops, or the Cardiff ones if you didn't mind bussing it twice a day, 'cause cars was as scarce as legs on lilies up our way; or there was the pit. The careers master plodded on, did old Moley, but for every Ton-y-Mynydd lad he tempted into going to University (about one in our year – forget all that *How Green was my Valley* rubbish) thirty more was equally divided between pit, shops and dole. And Willie wasn't much of a bright bean to begin with. However, when Moley asked him (fairly hopeless, I suppose) what his ambitions was, he sat up straight in his desk, wrinkled his forehead to show he was serious and said 'I got a plan, sir'.

Us lads stopped flicking bits of paper at Teresa-Marie Mulligan's perm and looked at him. Willie a plan? Never. Old Moley sneered and folded his arms.

'And what might that be, Probert? Please to share it with us, boy?' (In his Gwyn Thomas voice. Greatly admired Gwyn did Moley: fancied himself a bit of a raconteur.)

'Issa secret, Sir,' Willie mumbled, blushing.

Well, we all enjoyed the joshing that followed ('cept Willie, anyhow) and after the careers lesson a gang of us crowded round him in the yard trying to find out what the Secret Plan was, but Willie wasn't letting on.

But he lived by me, Willie did, just up the road with his batty Mam and his fat sister, and walking home after school, as a personal favour because he liked me, he told me. Honest, don't know how I kept a straight face.

'I'm gonna be a giggle-oh,' he confided, looking at his scuffed suede brothel-creepers.

'A what?' I asked.

'A giggle-oh. One of them men who gets paid for having thingy-aw, you know, Jonesey, ESS EE EX with women what can't get it, so they has to pay f'r it.'

I could feel my face turning purple, honest. Willie, a gigolo? He was tall enough, about six foot in his socks, but he was pale as a plate of spaghetti, and about as exciting. His muscles was like knots in a piece of string, and while he wasn't what you could call ugly, exactly, James Dean he was not either, if you get my drift. Nice teeth, but the acne didn't help. Willie, a gigolo?

We all idled on in school, pining for the day when the government would let us out, looking fairly hopelessly around for jobs and doing what came naturally for school kids in the fifties. I put the secret of Willie's big ambition aside until I needed it.

I needed it one musky summer evening up the Top, just as dusk was starting to close in, bats was wheeling out of the trees, and I was trying to get inside Teresa-Marie Mulligan's circle-stitched bra. I knew she'd let me, eventually, it was just a matter of technique and time. Oh, and bribery helped with Teresa-Marie.

'Go on, Ter, let me,' I mumbled, trying to get hold of the metal catch on her squirming back while simultaneously avoiding her slapping hands. 'I'll tell you what Willie Probert's Master Plan is.' She kept still long enough for me to get my hands on it. 'He never told you? Did he?' I nodded.

'I bet he never. Go on then, tell me.'

'Will you let me if I do?'

She tossed her head. 'Just for a minute – but you needn't think you can do it any time you want, after.'

A few seconds' manoeuvring and my hands, at least, was in paradise, and me with a silly grin that almost met round the back of my ears. I felt a bit dizzy, to be honest with you.

'Tell me then,' she insisted. So I did.

Her laughter echoed down the valley and back up the other side. 'What, Bloodless Bill? A fancy man for old bags what can't get it?'

I nodded. 'Why Bloodless Bill?' I asked, idly, my mind in my fingertips, but I have to admit I was a bit shocked when she told me, because I didn't think girls talked about things like that.

'Me and Sian and the girls decided that if Willie Probert ever got a hard-on, he'd prob'ly faint. There's not enough blood in him for both of 'em!'

Fair do's, though, Willie worked at it. He used to go down Ianto's Gym twice a week, regular, and boxed and worked out with weights, and ran everywhere. I used to go with him at first, but then I got a job in a men's outfitters down Cardiff and by the time the bus chugged into Ton at night I was too bloody knackered to do anything, not even wrestle with whichever girl was flavour of the month, although I did my best.

And Willie grew, and got some muscles, and collected his dole while he waited to put his master plan into operation. Whenever I saw him I'd say 'How's it going, Willie?' and he'd reply, puffing as he pounded past me, 'Gettin' there, butt, gettin' there.'

But I didn't see much chance of Willie Probert getting to be some rich bird's plaything.

Then the caff opened. Bracchi, of course – there's an unwritten law that any caff that opens in the Valleys is Italian. Luigi's it was called, although no one ever saw any Luigi, only Mrs Scarlatti and her daughter, Gina. And oh, God, wasn't Gina gorgeous?

Every lad in Ton-y-Mynydd spent every penny he had in Luigi's, just to catch a glimpse of that coffee-olive skin, those black-treacle eyes, that tumble of gleaming hair, and if you was really lucky, and didn't push it, like, those teeth. Oh, God, mun, those teeth! So white they almost had blue edges, like a nylon shirt under ultra-violet lights. They cried out, those teeth did, for the caress of a tongue, and the pressure of lips – mine, preferably!

Her Mam wasn't bad, either, but she was nothing up against Gina. To everyone, that is, except Willie.

Willie took one look at Mrs Scarlatti and found his heaven. And while we was all mooning hopeless over Gina, Willie moved in on her Mam. It wasn't until I noticed Willie's smug expression and satisfied grin that I actually took any notice of Mrs Scarlatti. She must have been in her thirties, looking back, although she seemed ancient to me, then. Black hair, nice complexion, big dark eyes like Gina's, and only the odd faint wrinkle round her eyes. Shaped OK, too, as far as you could see beneath the pink nylon overall. It was only her teeth, really, that spoiled her. Like Gina's they was small, white and even – but very, very pointed. She seemed to have only four square teeth in front, two top and two bottom: all the rest seemed to be canines.

If it had been me, now, I'd have had 'em fixed, whatdycallit, crowned, that's it. But it didn't make a bit of difference to Willie. Willie was hooked. I don't know how much of a living he was making as Mrs Scarlatti's toy boy, but he was well fed, well fixed and well f–. Well, he was happy, anyhow.

Then things seemed to happen very quickly. Gina married a boy from her village in Italy, and he come over to run the caff with her; strapping great bugger he was, which put paid to dreams of Gina.

Mama Scarlatti went to open another Luigi's somewhere else, and Willie and Teresa-Marie Mulligan disappeared. Oh, not together, not like that, but around the time Mrs Scarlatti left Ton-y-Mynydd, Willie packed his bags, kissed his Mam and sister, and took off as well.

Teresa-Marie – well, that was a mystery at first. No one knew where she'd gone. 'Course, first thing was she was knocked up and gone for an abortion, according to the rumour factory down the Co-op. Then it wasn't an abortion it was a kid, and then – then she turned up. Well, not Teresa-Marie, exactly, but all that was left of her. In the bushes up on the Top, where the wind screams down into the Valley, they found her, and I heard she looked as if a pack of dogs had been at her.

The *Echo's* headline was 'Terror of Ton-y-Mynydd' and the *News of the World's* 'Valleys Sex Beast Still at Large'. This was before bloody murders was as common as now, and it made more impact, like, especially in a little place like Ton-y-Mynydd.

The police interviewed nearly everyone in the village, but they didn't have nothing to go on, and no one was ever charged. Pushed her Mam right into the loony-bin, anyway, and her Dad had a stroke and died soon after, so there was no one local to keep nagging at the police to do something, like, so I suppose they sort of filed it away and forgot it for a bit.

I'd forgot it, too, until last week. I was up North on business – I'm a buyer for my menswear company now and married with three grown up kids of my own, and I was having a bit of a lonely wander round town before bedtime when I found a caff – a real old-fashioned Italian caff with a big chrome espresso machine hissing on the formica counter, and before I could make a conscious decision, I was inside, breathing the steamy, coffee-scented, smoky smell of my youth. And who should be behind the counter but Willie. But what a Willie!

He was big, and muscular, and he knew me in a minute. His face was tanned and his cheeks rosy – even his complexion had changed, and there was no trace of the acne'd, pathetic Bloodless Bill Teresa-Marie Mulligan and me had giggled over that night on the Top.

'Hello, butt!' he said, his face splitting in a delighted grin. 'Long time no see!' He reached his great hand over the counter and I grasped it. As our fingers touched, a figure came through the multicoloured curtain of plastic strips between the cafe and the kitchen.

They were still together. Mrs Scarlatti looked wonderful. I felt a definite twinge of envy – and something else besides – when I saw her, and it wasn't until much later that I worked out that if she was in her thirties in the Fifties she must be pushing seventy by now. She recognized me despite my beer-gut and thinning hair, and her red lips parted in a smile.

Willie said 'You remember Jonesy, don't you love? From Ton-y-Mynydd?'

'Of course!' she said, delight in her voice. There they stood, the pair of them, smiling at me, both looking impossibly young and healthy, the Ton-y-Mynydd Toyboy and his bit of ageing crumpet, and there wasn't a man alive who wouldn't have buckled at the knees at the sight of her.

I drank a cup of frothy coffee from a pyrex cup, then left the fragrant, nostalgic warmth with regret. It wasn't until much later, in bed in my hotel room that I realized what it was that was niggling at me, chewing at the back of my brain so sleep wouldn't come.

When they had smiled at me, Willie and Mama Scarlatti, side by side across the counter of their coffee shop, their teeth . . .

Their teeth had been identical: two straight, white, even teeth, top and bottom in front, and the rest, pointed, sharp, canine . . .

PARTIES IN BRIDGEND

~

Madeline Mayne

The bird had not burst into flame. He lay softly cold on her palm. She was telling him of the world they were in, strange, dark and without movement, sound or warmth.

She had been a little sick. No one had woken to clear it away.

'Enticed,' she murmured. 'Enticed.'

Siriol knelt at the kitchen table, becoming a snowgirl who was putting flour from a basin into the bowl of the food mixer. Nain said a snowgirl suited a day like Siberia. Nain was astonishingly small but did not have to kneel on the telephone directory on top of the kitchen stool.

Nain was a robin pecking busily about while Siriol worked.

If Nain was Mam's Mam – and probably not Dad's – was she Sian's Nain still, now that Sian had had a party to be grown up with, or was she Sian's Mam now?

Siriol had to stop being a snowgirl for a few minutes while the cake was being poured into its paper tin ready to be hidden in the oven. Then she could be a snowgirl again because she was putting lumps of icing sugar into the mixer bowl and it flew about beautifully. She licked her top lip.

'If I go to Coll in Bristol will Mam take me there?' – because how could she be taken up there and look after Nain all at the same time? She would not go if they made her blow her nose, like school.

Then Siriol had to stop being a snowgirl again because Nain was polishing her face for her and pulling her hair tidy. Nain was a great tidier and nothing lasted.

After the snowgirl had become a black girl with curly bark hair and the scuttles had been filled and the coalshed door closed, Nain polished and pulled her again. 'You're busy today, cariad.'

So Siberia had black trees and hard mud, with enough coldness to make Nain's nose as red as red, and in the evening became a place where snow came flying upside down, hissing its tiny hiss as it landed, tasting empty on the tongue.

Mam rang up. Was she helping Nain and being good? Yes, yes, snow in Bristol too, but not settling. Sian was in Coll and Mam and Dad would be back in time for tea, yes, special tea, tomorrow, Friday. Well, so old she no longer liked to think of it. You could not count it on one hand, like some people – this little pig went to market.

When Siriol woke the world up in the morning it was a different one, a shining, quiet one of snow sloping gently from the bedroom windows at the back and heaped into a mountain in the front garden. From upstairs she could see the top of it, smooth as ironing but not so flat. In this different world there was no coalshed, no bird table and most of the bushes had been taken away.

Siriol did an upside down snow dance that stopped suddenly because downstairs was like the coalhouse, dark and dark, with Nain fidgeting about with a funny lamp that came apart in the middle and had a cottony sort of bulb and a long shade made of glass that had to have a cloth pushed through it with a stick. The bulb came apart and a match lit the wire inside it. Then the cottony bulb burned black, but Nain turned the dimmer switch at the side and undid the burn.

'I've the fire to light before I can make the tea. The kettle's on stop. All the electric.' Nain gave Siriol her sugar crispies. 'When snow comes to this valley it certainly comes, but I've not seen the house half buried before, not in nearly sixty years.'

Siriol ate her sugar crispies. Nain lit the fire and put a saucepan on it and Siriol watched the flames sliding up the sides of the pan and peeping into it.

'When do we do Mum's birthday cake?' because it had been promised some snow of its own and there were no lumps in the icing sugar now.

'When the first thing's done and that thing is a way cleared to the coalshed,' – but that would spoil the beautiful snow. Then perhaps it wouldn't because the snow went up and up, right over the doorway, so they would make a snow tunnel.

'I've not seen it like this, even in '62. Taid was with me then, and not much more than youngsters – fifty seven and eight. Your Mam was married by then but your Uncle Haydn was here – no spade work left for us. Twenty years is twenty years.' She pushed a shovel into the snow wall. 'How can one rather small old lady and one even smaller young lady dig their way through this?' Nain shovelled into the wall, filling buckets and bowls which Siriol helped her carry through to the front door and out to the snow mountain. Her snowman would be climbing the mountain.

'Damn, it's cold.'

Siriol knew now that Nain was digging not for the coalshed but for a lifeline, which might be almost like it.

Whichever she wanted – and the coalshed was not there any more – the game went on too long. She liked it better when Nain stopped to show some tomato soup to the fire and make a ham sandwich each. Her nose had turned blue in the snow tunnel. After the soup it was white again. Then she went back to the tunnel and made the white nose red.

At teatime Nain had had enough, though it would have to be finished in the morning, by damn, so Siriol brought the cake out and they iced it while the fire licked its way across the lid of a saucepan and ate the handle in the middle. Mam had had to stop in Bridgened but that did not matter. There was too much to do to bother with Mam.

'Even the fire is hungrier than usual.' Nain put two logs onto it and the flames ran along the cracks in the bark and turned the little twigs into lamps.

'There'll be sheep trouble. Last time it was like this we still had sheep. Poor dabs! They scuttle to the hedge to get out of the wind and it drops all the snow on them there. The fox finds them if the farmer doesn't, and he keeps a good eye out until they are ready for him. You follow where Brer Fox goes. I remember once your Uncle Haydn . . .'

So the stories started and they sat and talked to the fire, with the cotton lamp beside them.

'. . . a real story, of magic and things.' Yes, Nain would, a story of snow, wolves and a witch, if that would do.

The witch was Baba Yaga, who lived in Russia 'Where it snows like this every year and they are used to it'. She had a hut with feet that could run away across the forest to find a better place – no, not on the corners, perhaps, but near the middle, yes, with little fur boots, just like those.

Yes, yes, she had done something she enjoyed, so you could be sure someone else would not be pleased about it, for that was what she liked – such as picking up the hot poker with little fingers that should not be meddling! – that was better. Baba Yaga had enticed away the magician's daughter to be her skivvy, not because she needed a skivvy but because the magician wanted his daughter to stay at home and do the washing up there.

A skivvy is someone who works in a kitchen, always doing

the washing up and never icing the cake. Yes, presently, they would boil some water and then they could wash up but someone's bones had too much cold in them yet.

The magician went hunting, hunting, for his daughter but as fast as he hunted just so fast did the little hut go running, running, while Baba Yaga sat in it and laughed – and the magician's daughter wondered how there could be so much work to do in such a teeny teeny house with only one old lady and one young one in it – but there always was.

Then the magician made a spell and all the snow in the world fell on to the little hut so it could not run any more. Then he sent wolves to prowl and howl around it. Well, Baba Yaga might have thought that they were all the wolves in the world but he would not have needed so many, would he, and what's the point of wasting magic?

The magician came knock, knock, knocking at the door. 'Daughter, your mother waits at home. The dough is proving at the fire. The samovar is ready. When I take you home the meal will be set,' – but all the girl heard was the wind singing in the trees and a bough knocking on the roof. He called again – well, he didn't know it was no good until he tried, did he? 'Daughter, your brothers wait at home. The goose is plucked. The herbs are in the pot. When I take you home the meal will be set,' – but all she heard was the wind sighing through the trees and a branch tap, tap against the window.

So the magician turned himself into a flake of snow and rode into the hut on the cat's twitch twitch tail, but Baba Yaga knew him and told the cat to swallow him. So he changed into a spider and ran up to the roof to spin a thread to catch his daughter and tie up old Baba Yaga – oh, very old – hundreds of years old. Before he had finished – no, not a long time – Baba Yaga had turned into a bird and flown up to the roof to eat him, but he threw the thread around her and changed back into himself to catch her – but still he had not won, for the bird's feathers changed into flames that went up through the roof of the little hut and all there was left was the magician and his daughter standing in the snow, while she wondered where all the washing up had got to – yes, we had better be getting on with it – oh, they rode off home on the backs of the wolves, because they belonged to the magician and he knew all their names – no, no, not now, if I ever did.

Siriol sack-walked her sleeping bag to the window in the morning and yes, they were there now, wolf tracks everywhere. Baba Yaga was up already, digging in the snow tunnel. 'Put your woolly pully on, cariad. The heaters didn't come on last night.'

The heaters were cold to the touch, colder than furniture. Siriol put her woolly on and went to talk to the fire which was telling her a story about a magnificent birthday party in a church hall at Bridgend, because Mam had said that there were hundreds of people there and none of them could go anywhere else because of the snow mountains. Mam was not dancing because now she was too old to do an upside down snow dance.

When the story was over Nain was still making the tunnel and would not stop to play with her. Siriol could see her from upstairs now, because there was no snow above the tunnel, which was a crack with Nain's red coat going up and down in it, like a flame.

At lunchtime Nain was cross, not with Siriol but with herself, because she had shovelled her leg and hurt it. '. . . had enough trouble without that'. Then she picked up the beautifully black saucepan to wash it and found it was full, because she had not given either of them lunch yet. She had to mutter some marvellous words and get the plates out again, because it was not the saucepan who was hungry.

The fire told more stories after lunch and this time Siriol drew them. When she had finished there was still Mam's birthday cake to look at. The icing was sweet as ever but like the snow, it held paw marks. She smoothed it nearly right again with her finger and went to help Nain carry buckets of snow again through the half-dark house. She piled it on to the climbing snowman. Nain or Mam would help her to make his head.

In the morning the snow was still there. Siriol came away from the window because the heater beneath it was still cold to the touch. Nain was up already and had gone to sleep in the chair.

The fire had no flames. When Siriol pushed the poker into it white ash flew on to her hand, leaving a black mark. She put the poker down and looked at Nain, who did not tell her she should not have touched it.

Perhaps Nain would like a cup of tea when she woke up. Siriol found the black saucepan with the half-eaten handle and climbed up to turn on the tap. She was not good at it, because no water came out, but she took the pan to the fire, anyway, carrying it carefully, without spilling.

As Nain was still asleep she poured her own sugar crispies and ate them with her fingers from the bowl and the table.

Perhaps Nain was having a headachy morning and needed a rug over her.

Siriol found one and tucked it carefully in under shoulders and elbows, and behind ankles and knees. It was difficult and took a long time. Then Nain was comfy. 'Good girl,' she said.

Siriol was doing her best. Nothing had happened to the saucepan so she took it off the fire.

She knew what Nain did to get the fire roaring, so she did the same things, screwing up the grey pages of the *Radio*

Times and pushing them among the cinders. There were no matches so she used Mam's trick of holding a paper to the bar of the electric fire. It did not light – perhaps because she had not asked permission first. She went up to Nain. 'Please may I light the fire?' Nain did not say 'No'. Siriol tried again. The she held a sheet of newspaper across the fireplace. Nothing changed. No flames went roaring up the chimney, shrinking a hole in the newspaper as they passed.

There must be something else she could do. She looked at Nain who still looked cold, as if she had just come in from shovelling snow. 'Shall I go and dig?' she asked.

'Yes,' said Nain. 'Put your red coat on, first, and your witch's boots.' So Siriol went to carry snow from the crack to the snowman without a head, but it was too hard without Nain and she would not know what to do with a lifeline, anyway, whether it looked like the coalshed that used to be there, or not.

She went to look at the wolf tracks. The poor little bird was lying just where a wolf would walk. He would feel safer indoors. 'May I keep him?' Nain did not say 'No'.

Siriol and the bird told each other stories until they were both hungry again. She looked round the kitchen. What should she do with all those things, potatoes with skins on and boxes of powdery things, like flour? There was the cake, of course, but she would have to ask first, because she did not want to shovel snow again. Mam had already had her birthday party in Bridgend, so she would not mind. She went to ask Nain, and to be quite sure, she climbed onto the arm of the chair and opened one of the stiff eyes. 'Do you mind if I have a piece of cake?'

She did not say 'No,' so Siriol and the bird went back to the kitchen. She had to eat partly from the plate and partly from the floor. She gave a piece to the bird and took some through to Nain, leaving it on the arm of the chair.

When Mam rang, Siriol told her Nain was asleep because she had a headache, but that only made Mam talk and talk until Siriol put the phone down on the table.

'I'm prickling,' said Siriol.

'Scratch your head, then,' said the bird.

'It's my knees,' said Siriol, 'behind them.'

'Then scratch those.' Siriol did so and had to lick her fingers afterwards.

Combing her hair was difficult. Perhaps it is easier if it is done in the morning. She ate some more cake. There was still Nain's piece left and the bit the bird had not eaten. She liked the fire better when it had flames. She put the bird to bed on a cushion because he was tired.

She told Mam on the phone that she had been sick but Mam only purred at her.

The noise outside was moving through the wolf tracks, pushing the snow aside. There were men with the noise, large men with loud red faces. Siriol did not want to know about them so she got into her sleeping bag. She could still hear them. Now they were in the house. Nain did not want to be woken up until her headache was better. The bird had a headache as well. Siriol started crying and took her tears to the very bottom of the sleeping bag.

The men made a noise everywhere. She heard them move the telephone.

'. . . like a bloody morgue . . . 'rything's on stop . . . too late . . . 'aven't found the child . . . must be he' . . . follow the tracks, then . . . wait for you out . . . after the sheep, if . . .'

There was quietness then and Siriol crept back up the sleeping bag, rubbing her tight, uncomfortable face. When she heard the car she turned the house round on its little furry boots to watch Mam arrive. It was not a car and it was not Mam. It was a landrover and a somebody who had no name. She made no noise at all, even when she saw Siriol and gave her a cup of tea from a thermos. She did not offer Nain a cup. Siriol thought of passing hers along but looked at the lady and changed her mind.

Later she said goodbye to Nain and kissed her and was carried away in a blanket, her hair tidied and her face rubbed clean, but not by red robin Nain, this time.

'That's the first time I've mopped up anyone's face with tea.'

'If the bird dies, can we bury it?' Yes, they could, under the snow. It wasn't far to the farm and it was warm there. Siriol could have a dish of cawl.

Nain would not like to be buried under the snow – unless it was tidied up again, afterwards, of course.

HOMECOMING

~

Christine Harrison

The nurses in the hospital seemed to be either angels or
devils. Pinioned as she was, and utterly reliant on these
white-winged attendants, she knew which ones wished her
well, and which did not. They came and went, day and night,
soft-footed, wings brushing against the bed. Sometimes one
was holding a silver tube or a draught of thick liquid in a
glass. Under their feathered wings were hypodermic syringes.
But crouched and coiled inside her all the time there was a
watcher who could tell at once whether their intention was
to help or to harm her.

If an angel approached, needle in hand, the drug released
into her bloodstream coursed with life-giving purpose. If a
devil stood, with cold eyes, offering small yellow tablets to
make her sleep, the coiled watcher inside unsprung to resist
those infernal dark tides. It struck and fought on her behalf.
Its energy came from inexhaustible sources and flayed with
intent ferocity.

At intervals she would be propped up against the pillows,
visitors circling her bed. The unaccustomed colours of their
clothes made her turn her head away. Their expressions were
wild, unpredictable and confused, their skins not pale, but
florid. They carried string bags stuffed with bright fruit; they
offered bunches of snapdragons and chattered of traffic jams.

Nevertheless they were uneasy and deferential to the
white-winged inhabitants of this ordered domain who before
long swept them out with their long wings, down the cool

corridors and out of the place. The jagged colour and noise drained away and left the ward cold, still and soundless again.

As Mrs Wilson got a little better she found it more difficult to tell the angel attendants from the devils. She was not sure any more. A smile could deceive her; a rough touch be misinterpreted. Still the watcher never slept and lay coiled inside her, seeming to sleep but ready to leap up and strike.

Once every day the consultant came round all the beds, attended by stiff-feathered nurses. Head on one side, he read charts and referred to files, totting up the scores to see which way things were going. Sometimes he took a brief, glancing look at the still figure on the bed, but the battle was being fought on his maps and charts. He held them in his hand, his fingernails gleaming with cleanliness.

His name was Mr Speering. This name was known to all. It was on everyone's lips.

One evening a witch-doctor burst his way into the ward. He stood in the middle of the room and danced, stamping strongly with his muscular legs, his tiger-clawed mantle ripped and in tatters. He whirled and stamped his wild but pre-ordained and strict dance. Only Mrs Wilson saw him. The other patients were asleep, but knew even in their sleep of his presence. Mrs Wilson knew that he was a witch-doctor and that his tiger skin, in any case, was in holes and tattered. She knew that the hospital would not have any truck with witch-doctors. They were not the fashion and were considered disreputable and unhygienic.

One morning Mrs Wilson was moved to another ward. Flowers stood about on the window-ledges. Beside the beds were little tables for fruit and water. The bedheads were rigged with headphones. The nurses had stopped appearing to her as beings from another world.

One was called Rose, she was Irish and had beautiful arched eyebrows; there was an aristocratic vagueness about the way she removed bedpans and administered injections. She seemed to be thinking of something else as she half looked at the thermometer and wrote something or other on the chart. Her gaze often wandered to the window as she searched the street below and the landscape beyond for something lost or someone who might return. She shook the thermometer with a listless air and carefully and slowly pinned her dark hair under the frilled cap. As she lifted Mrs Wilson on to her side, she would say, 'Mother of God. I wish they were all like you Mrs Wilson, you're as light as a feather.'

The sister on this ward was pale and sickly-looking. She had freckles and was very flat-chested under her nurse's apron bib. When she consulted the watch pinned on her flat chest she seemed like a little girl playing nurses. But her glance was cool and not childlike.

When it was time to change Mrs Wilson's dressing for the first time it was this sister who put the screens round the bed. Now the world, its shapes, its people stepped back. The pain spreading quickly, like a bloodstain, encompassed her narrowed world. Mr Speering's eyes were calm, they looked down on his handiwork. The nurses stood silent and stoic. Pain had a sound and smell, but she had not met them before. This was a country she had not known of, its dimensions and perspectives were different.

Afterwards she lay in the aftermath of pain, spent and relaxed. She put on her headphones. Music flooded her mind like a beam of light elucidating all the dark places.

It was Christmas Eve and Mrs Wilson watched the nurses putting up paper chains. These gave the tidy ward a childlike look. There was a Christmas tree, but no one had got round to decorating it. It was a tall, fresh-smelling dark evergreen, a gift from the Forestry Commission, said Rose.

Just before lights out the nurses came round the dimmed wards. They wore their red cloaks, red crosses over their breasts, lanterns in hand and sang. Their faces were grave and happy as they sang of angels and archangels. As they moved with gliding step on to the next ward, the quiet was broken only by a scuffling sound in the corridor outside and the urgent banging of the main swing doors.

On Christmas morning all the patients sat up like good children in bed. Only one patient did not sit up – she was new, she must have been brought in during the night and put in the bed next to the door. She lay still, her face and hands like dried leaves fallen on starched white bed linen. The face had an intent closed-in expression, an inward, strangely watching look.

Before she left the hospital Mr Speering explained to Mrs Wilson that she had only a few months to live and she might as well go home to her familiar surroundings. Several months had passed, they could do no more for her he said. He shook her hand but did not look at her. It was as if perhaps he had a sense of guilt for having diagnosed and discovered her malady, as if he had been the cause of it.

When she knew she had only a few months to live Mrs Wilson suddenly felt wide awake. She took a taxi home from hospital. Street lights glowing through an early evening mist made her flesh shiver with excitement. It was like waking to the clear real day of childhood; the intervening years distanced themselves like a dream. Pictures from early childhood flashed into her mind with a strange intensity. But a second later, almost simultaneously, despair and panic blocked her every escape. The black walls of the taxi encapsulated her, carrying her through the mournful streets, passers-by standing briefly by the kerbside.

Mrs Wilson's home was in a street of small houses. She did not know what the inside of any of the other houses was like. It was a necessity that those around her, sleeping by night so close – really only a few feet away behind the rose-papered wall – should keep their distance. The house itself was a close friend. She could feel her way about it in the dark. When she came home it greeted her. Sometimes she livened things up with a geranium in the window or a few autumn leaves on the table. The previous inhabitants of the old house often seemed to be there still, they went in and out of the doors; their faint presences skeined the house from corner to corner like a web of threads.

Now she sat at the kitchen table and told the house that she had only a short time to live. She put her head down on the table and wept, and then she howled like an animal in a trap. Her howls echoed through the house up into the empty rooms, they could have been heard all over the house.

She wiped her eyes with the tea-towel. Then she made some supper and went to bed. She slept peacefully.

When she woke next morning the sky was not quite light. Her room was further shadowed by lace curtains. Mrs Wilson slipped her feet onto the cold floor. In the half darkness and the coldness of the room every edge and surface and fold pierced her with excitement. It was like seeing the light of day for the first time. The world's dim shapes and outlines gradually became revealed in the strengthening light. She began to pack for a journey.

When she was packed she began tidying the house. It turned into something like a spring clean.

She wanted to get rid of everything that was no use to her any more. All the junk, the old letters, the clothes that didn't quite fit or she didn't like. A surge of energy went through her, she felt exhilarated as she discarded old cushions, piles of books. She put bags of stuff in the back of her battered van to take down to the Oxfam later on.

Then she made a cup of tea and took it out into the garden. She sat in the thin early morning sunshine and thought she was like one of those old photographs found in a box in the back bedroom. Sitting with her cup of tea by the stone wall. Soon you would be able to see the wall through her. See the sky and the stone through her. She sipped her tea and looked at the spiders spinning their webs in the Michaelmas daisies. She watched a wren pulling thistledown seeds from a dandelion.

How lovely a cup of tea was. What a nice morning too. A few dahlias left. Such brilliant colours, red and sharp greeny yellow. And a touch of frost on the grass.

It was time to set off on her journey.

It was in her mind's eye as she set off in her little van that she was making for a walled city. A medieval city, walled, spired and with close-packed houses. She followed the road out of town, past the High Street shops where she stopped briefly to leave the bags on the doorstep of the Oxfam shop. Her blue van sped through country lanes and out into open moorland. Here sheep and windblown crows claimed the rough country.

The van streaked between sky and earth. If she had wings she could have flown up into the cold harebell sky. A silver sun had light but little warmth in it, it frosted the skulls of sheep and sometimes a rib cage – all that remained of a once fleet wild pony.

Instead of a walled city she stopped to find lodging in a turreted small hotel. Inside it was like a stage set draped in gold-braided heavy maroon velvet curtains. These curtains lined the dining room and draped the little bar at one end of the room. The carpet was dull red and worn in places.

Her bedroom was in one of the turrets; because of this it was an odd shape. It was barely furnished with a narrow hard bed, a clothes press, a chair. Mrs Wilson opened the press. It was empty.

The place was very quiet. She had the feeling she was the only guest.

The sheets were tucked in very tightly. She could not concentrate on her book. Her hand shook a little as she switched out the light.

That night she dreamed she was driving across foggy moorland. Sometimes the headlights of the car transfixed a sheep's face looking towards her with a look of ghastly terror. The fog thickened so she could not see where she was driving at all, and at this point she gave up trying and the car seemed to be travelling of its own volition. At first this frightened her, then she let herself go with it. She woke feeling refreshed and rested.

After a while, lying there, she remembered Mr Speering. The doctor had smoothed down her file, pressing it down with his hands.

She did not stay for breakfast, but paid the bill and continued on her journey. She drove without thinking now, mechanically, it seemed as if she were driving but getting nowhere.

The doctor had held out his hand to shake hers. His hand had felt a little clammy, while hers had been dry and cool.

The wheels revolved and spun to no purpose, like running on the spot. Hitchhikers swayed at intervals. One made a flourishing sardonic bow as she drove past. She stopped.

He was a young black man of about nineteen. He wore a tiger skin under his old army coat. There was something of a jester about him, with his worn-down high heeled boots and his stylish walk, as if to music. He turned his eyes, downcast, thick-lashed, slightly bloodshot and glanced at her with a half smile.

When they reached a pub at a crossroads she said goodbye to him with assumed sangfroid for it was a tearing away, that particular farewell, and proceeded with her journey until nightfall.

Next morning a farm cock crowing woke her. It was still dark and if it were not for the harsh edgy excitement of the sound she would have fallen back to sleep. Outside, the first light of dawn cut the horizon with a sharp knife. She put on a warm coat and quietly opened the door of the unfamiliar ramshackle house. A night frost had sealed in the smell of the farmyard.

No eye watched her as she walked across stiff white grass, past village houses down to a steep path seawards. She stumbled down the sea path, the wide vista of sky, cliffs and darkly spreading sea rocking around her. Seagulls danced a wide dance across the sky. In the distance she saw two small figures making their way up the steep cliff from the beach. Tiny in the distance, bent forward with effort, two determined little two-legged creatures. Determined, assertive, extraordinarily brave and adventurous.

Her walk had given her a good appetite for breakfast. The tablecloth clean, crumpled; the bread warm and wholesome.

The farmer's wife came in with a tea-cosy for the brown teapot.

'Going far?' she asked.

'I'm not sure,' said Mrs Wilson.

'Come far?'

'Not very far.' Though it seemed it. After breakfast Mrs Wilson left her van in the farmyard and set out on foot to walk inland. Rosehips glittered in the hedge. From time to time she heard some small creature moving in the dry leaves. The road came at last to a sort of hill, or tor. She had to go down on all fours to reach the top. From there she could see for miles across country. It was exposed and windy, but she took off her coat and laid it on the ground. She swayed this way and that, held in the arms of the strong winds now blowing this way, now that. The sun was at its height now and shone down directly on her.

Quickly, like pulling off the outer layers from a dry, husky fruit, she took off her clothes. They lay all around her. Flowered blouse, skirt, silky underclothes, stockings and shoes all scattered round her and Mrs Wilson's thin, small body, silvery white in the sun, swayed like dry silky grass.

After a while her legs grew tired with the buffeting wind and she lay down in a little grassy hollow scooped out in the ground. She covered herself over with her coat. She felt very light, her heart beating against the earth. She fell asleep.

Mrs Wilson was glad to get home. As she went up the path she stopped to pick a few Michaelmas daisies. She noticed a half-grown angel strolling about, looking at the border of dahlias. It did not see her.

Inside the house, she put the daisies in a pot and set them right in the middle of the table. She told the house she had come back for a bit.

THE QUIET WATERS BY

~

Tessa Hadley

You wouldn't think it to look at me. Five foot three, seven stone, long wavy brown hair: if at a party a man asks me what I do you can see in his face he already thinks he knows the answer, I'm going to say I'm a housewife, or I work in an office, or I'm a primary teacher. I quite enjoy telling him I run my own security firm. As a rule that's the point he stops smiling at me as if I was some little soft furry thing he was about to pick up and put in his pocket.

I started off, at the time I was still with my husband, just breeding the dogs, German Shepherd dogs. I had to have something to do. Robert was away with the business all day, sometimes for days at a time. There was nothing to do in the house because with all the money he was making then we had a cleaner and a gardener, and anyway I've never really taken that much interest in where I lived, decorating and prettifying and tidying. It was a beautiful old Georgian house, even I could see that: built outside Bristol by the family of shipbuilders that had built the first iron-hulled steamship. Robert had collected all the old documents together, interested he said because he was connected with the shipping business himself: he bought up cargoes from ships in Avonmouth docks and resold them. When he first showed me round the house I knew that the girls I worked with then would have thought it was wonderful, and so I said I thought so too. He'd done it all up with his first wife; in the sitting room there was a bar covered with onyx with every kind of drink, and they had glassed over a whole central courtyard and filled it with hothouse plants. It only seemed to come to life, though, when there were guests: it was a strange place to be alone, as though you'd been left behind in a showroom after hours, by mistake.

I could have gone back to work at the building society after I was married. I had quite enjoyed my time there, the ritual of making your clothes and hair nice every morning, the work routines performed in a sort of mental gymnastics that didn't actually matter to you any more than throwing oranges in the air or balancing glasses of coloured water. But to go back just for the sake of it, now I didn't need the money, would have made it pointless, and anyway my life had changed, I couldn't really imagine myself sharing the same sort of colourless neutral gossip with the other girls. I had never even shown them, when I was still there, the emerald and platinum engagement ring Robert gave me, although I had thought I would, thought I'd present them my nicely manicured hand, turning it to flash the stone in cattish replete triumph as others had. But I was afraid of the ring with its too many, too-bright jewels and I kept it in a box in a drawer.

The funny thing was that I didn't like the dogs to begin with. There were two when I arrived, kept for security reasons. We'd never had dogs at home: like all little girls I'd pleaded for a puppy every Christmas, but as Daddy was bringing me up all alone and he was out at work all day while I was at school, it wouldn't have been fair. These two, Danny and Dolly, slightly disgusted me at first – I suppose I'd wanted a puppy with a ribbon around its neck – with their pink, wet gums, the threads of saliva vibrating between their teeth when their mouths were open, panting, and their wincing anxious hindquarters when they were given orders. But the dogs loved me, inexplicably, unencouraged. Robert was delighted with them, never stopped commenting on how they singled me out, how Danny waited hours for the privilege of laying a heavy head and a heavy paw on my lap, only withdrawing the paw and replacing it every so often, with an eye-rolling upwards glance, to remind me he was there. When I came back to the house after shopping or calling in on Daddy I played a game with them, altering whether I let myself in by the front, the back or the side door: unfailingly as I turned the key the dogs fetched up on the other side in a clatter of toenails on polished wood or vinolay. It was Robert's idea that I let Danny and Dolly breed, and sell the pups.

I had heating put in one of the old outbuildings that straggled off the side of the house, and later on when I had more dogs I made myself an office there too. I had a telephone and an electric kettle, and pinned on the wall the charts of pedigree I was learning about, records of inoculations, pricelists from the food wholesalers and so on. Although I was never short of business (the German Shepherds were getting more and more popular as guard dogs) I always found it restful in there: I was comfortable among the makeshift borrowed bits and pieces as I'd never been in the house, or even at home with Daddy. I had them bring across a big velvet armchair from one of the spare bedrooms: when I wasn't curled up in it one of the dogs was, and soon it was covered in hair: when I went back over to the house in the evenings I had to change my clothes and shower because Robert once complained I smelled of dogs. It was true they were always around me, I'd grown to like the feel of the presence of them, unintrusive, a paw on my knee, a strong panting flank against my calves where I sat sorting out my account book, the whistle of a snore from under the desk, the yap of the puppies from the kennels beyond, and the vigilant expectancy with which they all watched me for a sign that I was going to take them out for exercise.

As the numbers of dogs I kept increased, I had to pay a couple of schoolgirls to come up from the village in the evenings and help me walk them. They were nice girls, soft about animals in a way I've never been: they cried when we had to give away the pups, and imagined characters and feelings for the dogs as if they were humans. As a married woman with a business to run my experience was years apart from theirs, and yet at times we were cosily close: on autumn evenings, say, when we'd taken the dogs up Dunbury Hill and sat round afterwards in the kennels office, sharing a bar of chocolate and a pot of tea, all reluctant to leave the sleepy stuffy peace of the place.

'Did you see how Sasha wouldn't give me that stick, kept bringing it and then backing off with it? She's got a sense of humour, that dog, I swear it.'

'Look at Gyp, poor Gyp, he's tired out. He can hear we're talking about him – look, he's flicking his ears, but he hasn't even got the strength to lift up his head and look round. Eh, Gyp?'

I thought, this is what family life must be like, the talk going round in endless indolent comforting circles, like a dog treading down a place to sleep.

When I was a girl I never had close friends of my own age, my friends were Daddy's friends, and the conversation I knew was theirs, about house prices and promotions and gardening and cars and where to have furniture re-upholstered: there was gossip too, but all their rash acts seemed safely wrapped up in the past, only undone for talking over. Daddy encouraged me to bring home girls from school, but I thought they found me boring, with my grown-up person's ways. I suppose that was why I married a man so much older than myself: not one of Daddy's friends exactly, but I met him at a Christmas sherry party given by one of them. But he was different. They respected him, because of his money and his cleverness, and because his jesting bluntness always had public advantage over their careful manners. But he wasn't respectable: what he did was different to what we did, my father worked in an insurance office, we worked with papers and figures and notions, not things: what Robert did was buy up cargoes, of mango chutney, luminous paint, rice flour, anything going, at rock bottom prices because the original deals had fallen through, the stuff was perishable, and the ship in a hurry. Then he had it packaged, and resold it. It seemed to me then exotic. I suppose I was a little fool.

But he was the first one to make me feel a woman. He picked me out as soon as we came into the room, the morning of that Christmas party, and through all the smothering of women's kisses, and having my dress admired, and warming my hands at the log fire, and being found drinks and nuts, I knew that a man I had never seen before was waiting for his opportunity to come across to me, and sure enough he did, I felt him come although I didn't turn to see, and he asked our host to introduce him. What he said was nothing special – they all told me I was pretty, and I dressed up just like their women did, and made up my face like theirs – but he looked at me differently, and touched with a finger one of my earrings, pretending to admire it, and his small plump hand brushed my neck, and I remember how my face scalded. The sherry made me drunk, too, they didn't know how drunk: he teased me for blushing, me, when usually they marvelled at my coolness, and said that butter wouldn't melt in my mouth.

He wasn't handsome, oh no, in my daylight self I was

always half ashamed to have chosen him, he wasn't much taller than I was, and overweight, and his quickly expressive treacle-brown eyes and naked boy's pink face didn't correspond at all to the dignified reserve and five o'clock shadow that was the secret dream of the girls in the office. But I'd made up my mind, I couldn't help myself, even Daddy never tried to express any qualms to me before the wedding, Daddy with whom all my life I'd been so intimate, Daddy who'd taken me to the doctor's when I was a teenager and had trouble with my periods.

It was Robert who suggested that I should expand my business. For those first couple of years I was only a dog breeder: most of the sales I made were to the places where they trained them up and then resold them as guard dogs. But after a while it occurred to us that it would be much more efficient to breed and train the dogs in the same place. I did some homework, and then I tried it. Training begins as play, anyway. You use a padded arm first, for them to go for, and then a padded suit. Most private individuals only want dogs trained to the point of 'cornering' any intruder: usually in fact it's enough for the dog just to speak – to bark.

But it was only after Robert and I had separated that I began to operate as my own security firm. Suddenly I had a living to earn. Of course I got nothing from him, there was nothing left to get, the house had to be sold, and I used all Daddy's money to buy a new place for the kennels. It took a while for clients to accept me: fair enough, they asked for high level security, they didn't picture a woman, let alone five foot three. But I was quoting a very competitive price, so some of them took the risk. One of the first big contracts I got was at the racetrack at Silverstone. There I really did have a lot of trouble: I'd never have believed the lengths people would go to, to break in. One man didn't go when the dog spoke, he threatened it with a stick, challenging it: 'Come on then'. The dog felled him, and I radioed for help. I suppose he was drunk. I saw so much drunkeness there, the things some of them said to me I couldn't repeat: what growing up I had left to do happened there, pretty fast.

The contract I've got now is with a company building a new bypass; I patrol between six in the evening and midnight, I employ someone to take over until the morning. It's vandalism rather than theft that they're afraid of. Actually, I've hardly had any trouble, but it's a strange place to spend hour after hour. I'm never afraid, with the dogs, but sometimes I wonder what I'm doing there; nothing could be more desolate by night than the upheaval of that no-man's-land, the giant excavators and earth-movers like grazing monsters petrified in the act, the cold grave-smell of the earth turned up from underground, the flip-flap of the little plastic strips strung along nylon rope between stakes. The cleaners come in for a couple of hours to do the Portkabins, nice women, I look forward to the little bit of warm life they seem to make, not switching on the neon lights in the cabins – they're eerie, I prefer the dark – but the warmth of their voices, the slop of water in buckets, burr of vacuum cleaners, shuffle of flat feet. They always make me a cup of tea before they go. The one who brings it out to me is Jean, soft and shapeless as a pillow buttoned into an overall, the orange point of a cigarette-end advancing through the dark. Some of the remarks they swap around are pretty blue, but it's never like with men, I never mind them somehow.

When they go, at nine, I have to be brisk with myself. The dogs and I set off on a tour round. The great thing is not to let the influence of the place inside. Once you begin to think it's inside, the upheaval, the emptiness, you've got trouble. I sing. Pop songs, songs from musicals, hymns, the twenty-third psalm: I've not got much of a voice, but who cares? By rights, there shouldn't be anybody listening.

These days, you don't know what to be afraid of – you'd have to do the job I do to believe some of the things I've seen. You don't know where fear's going to come from. I thought I was safe – I was certainly never afraid of losing the money, the house – but in the end there was nothing to protect me from myself.

It was when Daddy died. I knew things were wrong with Robert's business, I suppose I knew really that the whole thing was going to come tumbling down about our ears. We never talked about it, but there were enough letters and telephone calls, a lot of them from solicitors, and anyway I'd never lost that instinct I had with him, not quite as if he was transparent, more as if in his presence I was so empty of myself I felt on my skin what he was thinking. In the same way I knew he'd been unfaithful, too, and had been sure with a shock once or twice, when he kissed the top of my head affectionately coming in to breakfast, that he'd been late home the night before because he'd been making love to some other woman. It didn't seem to matter. I accepted everything he did, as if I'd deliberately put myself under his spell and didn't want to wake up. I knew I was prettier and younger than any others he was likely to get, anyway – I could see that in the way he looked at me – and so, like a fool, I thought I had him safe.

The day Daddy's neighbour phoned me to say that Daddy had had a heart attack and been taken into hospital, it happened that my car was in the garage having the clutch fixed, and Pam, who was working for me full-time by then, had taken the van into Bristol to stock up at the wholesalers. I had been working with the dogs. I don't know why I panicked: it wasn't Daddy, it was the idea that I was all alone at that place and couldn't get out. It had never occurred to me all morning while I was busy, but as soon as I wanted to go, the not having a car was horrible, like a paralysis.

I should have phoned for a taxi, but the idea didn't come into my head. Without stopping to think I tried to get Robert at the offices, Robert at the docks. Then I convinced myself that he would be at his solicitors, but I had no idea of the number. I raced up to the house, and went through the personal phone book with desperately clumsy fingers, couldn't find it. The urgent need to get to the hospital transformed into the need to find Robert.

Yvonne's – his first wife's – number had always been in the book. I'd never spoken to her, although I had known her by sight before I met Robert. Of course he had to keep in touch with her over the boy, and they still had business connections. They'd built the business up together, he'd separated off certain areas and given them over to her on the divorce. I thought with the zig-zag rationale of panic that she would be able to give me Robert's solicitors' number.

Her voice was a shock. Her accent was broad Bristolian, like Robert's: surly, ironic, just how he answered the phone. She was suddenly real – and calm – instead of a figment of my purpose. I hadn't really expected her to be in, to exist at the end of a number scribbled in a book.

'Yvonne? It's Helen. I need to get in touch with Robert.' I felt the words folding up on my lips, prim and hollow as a schoolgirl's. 'I thought he might be at his solicitors, and I don't have their number.'

'You're looking for Robert?'

'Yes, it's urgent. I'm stuck here without a car and I've got to get out.'

I felt her pause, enjoying the unexpected, and hearing her voice triggered a precise memory of her I hadn't known I'd kept. Fat plain face with dabs of blue on the eyelids not meant as embellishments, only concessions to a social occasion; brusque small red hands; a settling, complacent gesture of drawing her chin back each time after she spoke.

'Just a moment. I'd better get him for you.' Before I knew what she had said she added, 'He's just been lying down'.

I was so astonished I almost giggled, and when after a few moments Robert suspiciously said hello into the phone I simply delivered my message without comment and told him I expected him back to take me to the hospital in half an hour. Then when I had replaced the receiver I curled myself into a ball on the hall floor, hugging my knees, because my heart wouldn't beat, and when it did it beat so thickly I thought it was going to burst with blood. I had to force myself to breathe in, like tearing open something suffocating me.

He came, he took me to the hospital. Daddy had died and I couldn't even take it in, I didn't cry. On the way home he wanted to explain why he had been lying down at Yvonne's and I wouldn't let him. What drove me almost mad as I sat beside him and he susbsided into his own thoughts was that I couldn't feel them any more. I had no idea whether he was thinking of me, and Daddy, or if I was the least of his problems.

He didn't offer to explain again. He went upstairs when we got home and ran a bath, and I stood where I had taken off my coat and listened: what did he expect me to *do*, physically, what was there left to do, now?

So I took his airgun down from where he kept it in a locked cupboard, loaded it – he'd shown me how to do it – and went up to his bathroom with the champagne-coloured suite and one of those sunken baths with a jacuzzi. He looked pink and foolish, naked in the water. He said something like, 'My

God, Helen, you can't be serious,' and then I pointed the gun and shot at him.

I'd never shot a gun in my life before and hadn't got a clue. The moment after the explosion it was me that burst into tears – and I heard all the dogs begin to bark – at the sight of the pink blood in the water and on him, while he was scrambling out and wrapping a towel round his arm, and telling me calmly, although I heard the tremor in his voice, to go and call the ambulance.

Thank God I didn't hurt him much. They didn't even keep him in hospital overnight, he went to Yvonne's and she nursed him. It didn't matter any more: what could have been more natural than his going with all his troubles to his friend who was like him? I didn't even know afterwards why I'd minded so much.

I took a duvet and a piece of foam over to the office and slept on the floor there, that first night, and in the weeks afterwards before the house was sold. The dogs welcomed me, licking my hands and face joyously, as if nothing had happened, and I was grateful to them.

It was Robert who had to go to prison, and not me. They did him for tax fraud. On my behalf, over the shooting, they pleaded mitigating circumstances and temporary imbalance of mind. I've moved far enough away for the story not to follow me. But I don't forget, not ever for one moment. Who can you trust if you can't even trust yourself?

I trust my dogs, one hundred and fifty percent. Sometimes I'm sorry that I haven't had children. I can imagine what it would feel like: you feel something, even for the puppies, warm, tender, tugging, softening. But I'm not sure it isn't for the best. Other times I think this isn't a world to bring children into.

COLD HANDS, WARM HEART

~

Janet Thomas

Beth glanced across at the recipe book for reassurance. Taking her courage in her hands, she poured the warm water into the middle of the flour, salt, butter and yeast. It looked far too much. Small peaks of flour emerged from the pool like mini icebergs. The water went a flat, grey-beige colour. A dead colour. Pulling a face, Beth plunged her hands in and started to mix.

The table was a little too low for cooking. Her back twinged slightly as she bent. She was supposed to stir this with her hands, according to the instructions, but her fingers just clagged up with gunge. She dragged them out. They were so covered they looked as if they were melting. They made her think of the witch in *The Wizard of Oz*. Witches were always blamed if a woman turned out to be barren, weren't they. She wished she could pick some old biddy to blame.

She had to stop thinking like this. The bread was going wrong already. It looked like wallpaper paste. A stray tear leaked from nowhere and splashed into the goo. Closing her eyes, she leaned over the table, aching, swearwords souring the back of her throat. This had to work. She needed it. She needed it so much.

Since Beth had had the results, it was as if something inside her had broken. She knew it wasn't rational. It was like being haunted. Her plants had come down with a white mould, as if it had been snowing inside the house. The cat had started being sick – on the chairs, the stairs, the bed – and the vet couldn't find anything wrong with him. Beth's cooking fought back at her, burning, boiling over or just refusing to bind. The Indian, Chinese and chippie now knew Jack by name.

For the first time in her life, she couldn't walk under ladders and was throwing salt over her shoulder at any excuse. She'd tried telling Jack she felt as if something had happened to her, something primeval, primitive, but she couldn't explain it right. The next time they went to the clinic, he'd asked Dr Roberts if the drugs resulted in any side effects, like paranoia or hallucinations. Beth just had to laugh.

Talking to Jack about anything was just too difficult at the moment.

She tore the mixture off her fingers and slowly sank her hands back in for another go. She began pressing it down with the heel of her hand, turning and pressing, turning and pressing, making a torn, raggedy ball.

She'd been in the clinic yesterday, lying there with her legs in the air, like an acrobat frozen half way through a trick. They were harvesting the eggs. Tears rolled from the corners of her eyes straight down cold into her ears, as she stared at the ceiling and tried to distract herself. Eggs, she thought. She imagined the egg-shaped stomach she wanted, imagined smoothing her hands over it. Imagined the baby fighting its way out. God, that would be more doctors and tests and her body stretched out for public view. Why didn't she just give up now, go back to normal?

There was no answer for that. Think about something else.

Eggs. One of the reasons her cooking had gone crazy was that she couldn't crack eggs any more. They made her cry. The white, slippery and sinuous as bodily fluids, the brash yolk, the stringy black fleck of life. Scrambled, boiled, poached, fried, coddled, over-easy – how spendthrift we were with life.

'Nearly there,' the doctor called, looking up from between her thighs.

This is a kind of cooking, Beth thought. First catch your mother. Marinade her in hormones. Stir up the husband in a completely separate bowl. Mix together carefully. Here's two we froze earlier.

She laughed out loud for a second and all the nurses looked at her.

Think about something else.

Lying there, she'd decided she needed to do something. Something she could create, something to make her feel connected again. And she'd thought of bread. The staff of life. The live yeast, bubbling and breathing. She would make bread. She hadn't tried since she was a child, but there was something mystical about bread. It would restore her faith in herself. On the way back, she'd made Jack stop at the supermarket for flour and yeast. She'd wanted the sort that would fizz up in a jug, but they only had dried, so that had to do.

Supermarkets are full of children.

So here she was. It was almost all mixed together now, with only a few scraps stuck to the bottom of the bowl. She floured her board and emptied the heavy lump on to the table. The bang rattled the kitchen. She'd been looking forward to the next bit, rubbing the crust of dough off her hands as she checked the book again. Press in with the base of the palm. Fold the sides into the middle. She timed herself for ten minutes, as it said on the yeast packet. 'Enjoy the kneading,' the book said. 'Think of something that is frustrating you.' They didn't have to ask twice.

Thump, thump. That was for the medical staff. Of course

they were kind and she was lucky they could help her at all, but they made her feel so passive. She was the stupid kid kept back after class because she couldn't get this basic lesson through her thick head.

Press down, fold and press. That was for her mother. All those concerned phone calls, the frowns, the over-cheerful, 'not the end of the world' advice.

She turned it and dug her knuckles in, leaving squashy dimples. Thump. That was for Katie, who ducked away from Beth, shrouded in embarrassment, since she'd got pregnant. What did she think Beth was going to do to her?

Thump, pound, tug. That was for Jack, who moved so quietly about the house, haunting her with his own heavy disappointment. Who was so careful with her he just made her feel more broken. Who was frightening her, the way he'd started coming home later and later.

And that – she picked the dough up and threw it back down on the board, making the table shiver – that was for her own flesh, her own useless, treacherous body, which had put her through seventeen year of periods and spots and fat thighs and taking the pill and PMT and cramps, all for this nothing. This refusal. She wanted to fling the dough about the room, rip it apart, tear it to dust.

The timer rang, making her jump. Was the dough ready? It was the colour of flesh now, flesh that needed a bit of sun. It felt heavy in her hands, springy and pliable. She squeezed it and the feeling gave her satisfaction.

Putting it down on the table, she stared at it. A moment ago she'd wanted to destroy it. What did she feel now?

Carefully, tenderly, she folded the ends into the centre, turning it over and easing it into the bowl, so that it was a smooth circle, slightly dimpled, like a round belly. She put oiled clingfilm over the top and chose the work surface by the cooker as the warmest place for it to rest.

She just stood over it for a moment, but there was nothing more to do except wait. The yeast packet said she had to leave it an hour and a half to prove. She stayed there a moment, shifting her weight from foot to foot, but there just wasn't anything else she could think of to do.

Setting the timer for an hour and a half, she carried the clock through to the living room and eased her back into an armchair. Her upper arms were protesting slightly at the unusual exercise. She kicked her shoes off. She'd thought she'd half-read, half-worry, but after a moment the book slipped from her fingers. Sleep eased itself over her gently, like a warm cloth. Couldn't worry about the bread now, she thought, as she drifted away. Done all I can. Just have to let what happens, happen.

She was so tired of worrying.

As she slept, the soft, warm smell of yeast rose through the house like sunlight.

BIOGRAPHICAL NOTES

ELIZABETH BAINES is the pen name of Helen Johnson, who was born in Bridgend, spent her early childhood in Wales, and studied at Bangor. She is the author of many published short stories and the novels *The Birth Machine* (The Women's Press, 1983) and *Body Cuts* (Pandora, 1988), as well as an award-winning radio playwright. She now lives in Manchester.

PAT BONNELL was born in Swansea and is a graduate of University College, Cardiff. For many years she taught religious studies but has recently devoted much of her time to writing. Several of her short stories have been successful in competitions and have been published in anthologies. She is currently working on her fifth novel.

KAY BRYLEWSKI was born in Aberafon. She trained as a radio operator with the Air Force, where she met and married a Polish flier. After leaving the service they settled in Cambridge, though she has never relinquished her close links with Wales. Her work has appeared in *Cambrensis, QWF, Home and Country* and on BBC radio.

TESSA HADLEY was born in Bristol in 1956 and read English at Cambridge. She then went on to graduate with an MA in Creative Writing from Bath Spa University College. She now teaches literature full time at Bath College and is researching a PhD thesis on Henry James. She has lived in Cardiff for the past fifteen years.

CHRISTINE HARRISON was born on the Isle of Wight and lived in many different places before moving to Fishguard over twenty years ago. There she began writing short stories, winning several awards, notably the Cosmopolitan Short Story Award. In 1991 she was the recipient of a writer's bursary from the Welsh Arts Council. Her novel *Airy Cages* was published by Macmillan in 1994, and she is currently working on a collection of her short stories.

JO HUGHES was born in Swansea in 1956 and has lived in Aberystwyth and London. Her stories have been broadcast on Radio 4 and published in various magazines and anthologies. She was one of the winners of the Rhys Davies Short Story Competition in 1995 and her story 'Too Perfect' appeared in the competition anthology, *Tilting at Windmills* (Parthian). 'Mistaken Identity' was shortlisted for the Asham Award.

MADELINE MAYNE was born in the East Riding of Yorkshire and brought up in the Yorkshire Dales. She studied medicine at Bristol University and went on to qualify and to practice medicine in Wales until she retired in 1984. Her poems and short stories have been widely published and anthologized in magazines and on the radio. Her novel, *The Lord Sun*, was published by Macmillan in 1986.

CLARE MORGAN was born in Monmouthshire. She has published a novel, *A Touch of the Other* (Gollancz) and many short stories, some of which have appeared in *The New Penguin Book of Welsh Short Stories* (1993), the British Council anthology *New Writing*, Malcom Bradbury's *Classwork* (1996), and on Radio 4. Her collection of stories *An Affair of the Heart* was published by Seren in 1996. She lectures in

English Literature at Christ Church, Oxford, and divides her time between Dinas Mawddwy, Oxford and London.

SUSAN MORGAN was born in Uganda in 1956 and lived in Australia before moving with her family to Swansea. She studied English at Sussex University and then taught English and Drama at schools near Brighton. Since moving to Cardiff eight years ago she has been writing poetry and is currently writing a radio play for Radio 4. 'Fog' is her first published short story.

JENNY SULLIVAN was born in Cardiff but now lives in Raglan. Having left school at 15 she returned to education in 1993 and graduated with an MA in Creative Writing from the University of Wales, Cardiff, where she is currently researching her PhD. She has written four novels for children, one of which, *The Island of Summer,* was highly commended for the Books Council of Wales Tir na nOg Award in 1997. A fifth novel, *Following Blue Water*, is forthcoming from Pont.

JANET THOMAS was born in Aberystwyth in 1967. After studying English at University College London she worked for Hodder & Stoughton Children's Books. She has now returned home to Aberystwyth, where she works as a freelance editor and proof reader, and is writing her first novel. *Cold Hands, Warm Heart* is her first published story.

ALEXANDRA WARD hails from south Wales and now lives in Llanfihangel y Creuddyn in Ceredigion. Her serious education began in the late sixties when she became a student at Coleg Harlech: from there she went on to University College, Cardiff and did research at the University of East

Anglia. Her short stories have appeared in Honno's previous anthology *Luminous and Forlorn* (1994) and the *New Welsh Review.* She is a descendant of Lucy Thomas, Abercanaid, a pioneer of the Welsh coal industry.

SHELAGH WEEKS was born in Bristol in 1956. She lived in Cambridge and Devon before moving to Cardiff in 1992. She currently teaches literature at the University of Cardiff Department of Continuing Education and is a reader for the BBC Wales radio drama department. 'A Dangerous Dance' is her first short story to be published.

NIA WILLIAMS was born in Cardiff in 1961 and studied History at the University of Exeter and European Studies at Reading. Her short stories have been published in *Cambrensis* magazine and the anthology *Tilting at Windmills* (Parthian) as well as broadcast on Radio 4. She has recently moved to Nottinghamshire, where she works as a freelance writer and editor and is currently working on a radio play.

ABOUT HONNO

Honno Welsh Women's Press was set up in 1986 by a group of women who felt strongly that women in Wales needed wider opportunities to see their writing in print and to become involved in the publishing process. Our aim is to publish books by, and for, the women of Wales, and our brief encompasses fiction, poetry, children's books, auto-biographical writing and reprints of classic titles in English and Welsh.

Honno is registered as a community co-operative and so far we have raised capital by selling shares at £5 a time to over 350 interested women all over the world. Any profit we make goes towards the cost of future publications. We hope that many more women will be able to help us in this way. Shareholders' liability is limited to the amount invested, and each shareholder, regardless of the number of shares held, will have her say in the company and a vote at the AGM. To buy shares or to receive further information about forthcoming publications, please write to Honno, 'Ailsa Craig', Heol y Cawl, Dinas Powys, Bro Morgannwg CF64 4AH.

ALSO FROM HONNO

Of Sons and Stars
by Catherine Merriman

Judith was undressing on Friday night in front of her long bedroom mirror when she realized – with a shock that momentarily paralyzed her – that she had become invisible.

Bikers partying in a remote mountain pub; an Englishman in search of mustard in a quiet Welsh village; a housewife whose perfectly ordinary life suddenly becomes very strange indeed . . . Catherine Merriman's stories take everyday reality and give it a twist and a spin, transforming it into something bright, shiny and with a definite edge.

Catherine Merriman is the author of three highly praised novels, the first of which, *Leaving the Light On* (Gollancz/ Pan), won the Ruth Hadden Memorial Award. Her first collection of short stories, *Silly Mothers*, was shortlisted for the Welsh Book of the Year Award, and is also available from Honno.

I would say this author is born to write – Lynne Reid Banks.

£5.95

ISBN 1 870206 27 4